Dark Rendezvous

Bob Killebrew

 Blue Dragon Publishing

Published by Blue Dragon Publishing, LLC
Williamsburg, VA
www.blue-dragon-publishing.com
Copyright © 2019 by Bob Killebrew

ISBN 978-1-939696-52-6 (paperback)
ISBN 978-1-939696-56-4 (epub)
Library of Congress Control Number: 2019915787

Cover by Resa Reid

Printed in the U.S.A

Dedication

To Pixie… for all the late nights

Chapter 1

January

Fedor got the call the second week of January, after the hard freeze. The thirty-year-old was rough shaven and shabby, with the sallow complexion that comes from bad nutrition and too much alcohol. His eyes, usually drab and dull, were now feverishly bright as he hung up the phone.

"It is time. Viktor says it must be now," he said to his partners.

"He wants it now?" Georgy asked. "This is sudden."

Compared to Fedor's stocky and dark presence, Georgy was thin and blond with a wispy beard, bad complexion, and hesitant manner. He flopped down on the edge of the bed next to his girlfriend.

Valerlya rose to her knees, slipping her slim arms around his shoulders and pressing her breasts against his back.

"It's the call we've been waiting for," Fedor said, irritated by the hesitation in Georgy's voice. "This will make us rich!" After the months of waiting, he struggled to contain his excitement.

Georgy caressed Valerlya's arm. "You should wait for us here. We won't be gone long."

"Don't be stupid," she replied. "I'm not going to miss out on the fun."

He turned to look her in the eyes. "You should wait."

She pushed her lower lip out in a pout that looked incredibly childish on a twenty-something. Georgy kissed her anyway.

"Very well, but you will wait in the car. This is no place for you."

"Enough already," Fedor said impatiently. "Let's move."

~

The Russian night was dark and cold, with a foot of snow already on the ground and more on the way. No other cars dared the one-lane blacktop. The road went from bad to worse as Fedor turned the car off the pavement, bounced onto a rutted, frozen track, and turned off the headlights.

As Fedor slowed the car, Georgy pushed open the creaking door of the old Fiat and emerged to walk ahead of the darkened car as it crept into the grove of dark pines. Holding a dim flashlight pointed at the ground, he led the car to an opening in the brush a kilometer from the front gate of the old plant, but only a few meters from the rusted perimeter fence, out of sight from the gate and the road. Wordlessly, Fedor killed the engine and got out, the creak of the door loud in the silence.

The snow wasn't as thick under the trees, but his boots still left tracks as he walked around to the trunk where Georgy joined him. Together they hoisted out the two rucksacks holding the tools Viktor had instructed them to bring.

Leaving the trunk lid ajar and Valerlya wrapped in blankets in the back seat, the men walked without speaking through the darkness and pristine snow to the rusted remains of the old double-strand security fence.

Fedor hoped Georgy couldn't hear his racing heartbeat. He didn't want to give Georgy any reason to suspect his unease about this mission. It seemed too easy, with Viktor dictating their every move and anticipating their needs. Viktor was a controller, Fedor knew, but this made him less comfortable, not more.

Viktor said the fence would not be an obstacle, and it was not. With little effort, they pushed through both fences and the tangles of barbed wire, unaware of the old mines and booby traps that had long since decayed. For long minutes they were exposed on the open ground, but the guards were in their warm offices with their bottles and television.

Finally, the old warehouse loomed in the darkness, just as Viktor had said, its main structure built securely on a massive concrete slab. Easing to the side, as he had directed, they located the office building, a later addition built with a wooden floor on stringers. Beneath the floor was a crawl space sealed off with simple wire fencing.

The two men seized the rusted wire, which gave way with a strong tug. Bending the corroded metal back, they entered the crawl space under the building and bent the opening closed behind them. Finding a spot toward the middle of the cramped space, they emptied the tools from the rucksacks they carried. Counting on distance to conceal the noise of his battery-operated drill and saw, Georgy quickly cut through the crumbling wood floor of the office extension while Fedor held the shrouded light.

Once the hole was large enough, they pulled themselves into the darkness of a hallway inside the building, and with some effort, found the door Viktor had described. With a single sharp blow, they knocked the rusted lock off with the sledgehammer that Georgy carried. Pushing open the squeaking door, they saw a row of waist-high steel containers shining dimly in the pale light. *Viktor was right again*, Fedor thought. *He knows more than he is telling.*

Fedor had met Viktor on a trip to Rostov to visit a distant cousin. The cousin, a young man of no special talent, had drifted into shakedown work for Viktor, who had the nice car, western clothes, and expensive tastes of a made man.

Viktor paid no attention to Fedor, a yokel from the backwoods of southern Russia, until the younger man mentioned Palaskova. Viktor knew the shithole that was Palaskova and knew about the old Stalin-era atomic plant on the outside of town. Before the Soviet Union collapsed, when Viktor was young and hard, he had been a major in the KGB's special security branch, responsible for nuclear security. He was intimately aware of the failures of the Palaskova plant's security system.

When Fedor mentioned the plant was largely abandoned except for a few lazy guards, Viktor had gotten interested in Fedor. Over several days, the older man brought him into his confidence as the cousin was edged out. Finally, one alcohol-fueled night, Viktor closed the deal.

"You want out of Palaskova, don't you?" he asked Fedor.

"Of course," the young man said, sensing an opportunity.

"I can make you a rich man. Rich enough to get out and never go back."

Fedor looked at him doubtfully.

"No, no. There is very little risk," Viktor assured him. "If the things you have told me are true, we can both get rich with some materiel I know is still inside one of the old warehouses. I know how to get in and out of the old plant undetected. And I know how to sell what you bring me and make us both wealthy men." He lowered his voice. "I too want to go to the West as a wealthy man. We can do it together."

After a moment, Fedor nodded. *The West.* Visions of blue jeans and shopping malls filled his mind.

Viktor smiled and made rough sketches of the clusters of old buildings in the factory complex on paper. Pointing at the largest one, he said, "Here is where you need to go." He spent the next twenty minutes explaining what Fedor would need to get into the building and what he would find inside. "I will get you a list of the things you need to take, but don't move until I say. Do you understand?"

"I understand," Fedor assured him. He had no intention of crossing this man. Easier to do the grunt work and get paid well.

"And only take what I tell you, no more. The guards probably do not know what they are guarding, but do not get greedy," Viktor said.

"If the things you want me to get are heavy, it will be easier with another person. I can get someone I trust," Fedor offered.

"Do you trust him with your life?"

"Yes."

"Then I approve. But do not discuss this with anyone else. The fewer who know, the smaller the risk," Viktor said.

Fedor had returned to Palaskova with a mind afire with ambition. He immediately brought his friend Georgy into the plot, but Georgy insisted on bringing Valerlya. Fedor couldn't say no. He had already told Georgy the plan. If Georgy backed out, Fedor would have to tell someone else what they were planning. Either way, it would mean a third person knowing. At least, he thought, Valerlya was too stupid to ask questions. And she was as desperate as they were to escape the Russian backwoods before she became old and dumpy like the other women of the town.

Now as they positioned the empty canvas bags on the floor, Fedor prayed they would get what they came for quickly and without incident. He stepped forward to grasp the first of the containers Viktor had described. After some trial and error, he managed to unclip the top, twist it off, and set it aside. With a racing heart, he looked inside, but what he saw in the dim light of the shielded lantern was anticlimactic.

"What is it?" Georgy asked, pushing Fedor aside to look. Fedor pushed him away, reached into the container, and pulled out a rectangular, brick-sized object wrapped in heavy, tarred paper and bound with steel wire.

"Fedor, is this—"

"It is, you fool! Keep silent."

Fedor picked up another brick from the stack, surprised by its weight. It had to be over twelve kilos. He handed it to Georgy, who placed it in the first rucksack. Working silently, they loaded three bricks each into the two rucksacks. Carrying them awkwardly, they made their way back to the hole in the floor and dropped through.

In the tight crawl space, they dragged the bags across the ground to the opening in the wire fencing. Cautiously they scanned the area around the silent buildings for guards. There was no movement. They pulled the packs out, bent the wire back into place around the opening, raised the heavy rucksacks to their shoulders, and retraced their footsteps through the snow to the car where Valerlya waited, shivering under her blankets.

"Holy God," she whispered through chattering teeth. "I thought you would never return. Here." She offered the two men the bottle of vodka she had obviously been nursing. "Warm your blood."

Each took a pull, then wordlessly unloaded the bricks into the trunk, wrapping them in the blankets they had brought for the job.

"We must return but only for one more load," Georgy said.

"Fine," said Valerlya. "But do not take so long. My feet are frozen." She tipped the half-empty bottle to her lips again.

The men retraced their steps through the pines and across the field. Snow fell heavily now, and the tracks from their first visit were already indistinct. They bent the same wire back and reentered the building through the hole in the floor. Fedor opened the second cylinder in line. Wordlessly, he and Georgy removed six bricks from the cylinder and divided them into the rucksacks, as before.

Georgy reached for a seventh brick.

"No. Can't you follow simple instructions? Viktor said no more than twelve," Fedor whispered.

"How will he know? It isn't like he's going to come check. We can keep this for ourselves."

"And what would we do with it? We don't have the connections Viktor does. Besides, somehow he would find out," Fedor said, taking the brick from Georgy and placing it carefully back into the cylinder. "I'm not taking any chances." The cold night, the weight of the rucksacks, and the tension had exhausted him.

Georgy wordlessly agreed. As they left the shelter of the building, they carefully bent the fencing under the building back to its original position and after a final furtive look around, they walked away from the warehouse as before. Bent under the weight of the heavy rucksacks, they made no effort to brush their tracks away. The falling snow would finish the job before daylight came.

By dawn, they were in Valerlya's flat, and the bricks were in two old footlockers hidden in a shed outside. While the three of them drank and slept away the labors of the night, the drifting snow piled up to the eaves of the shed, and all traces of their theft were erased.

Chapter 2

Early February

Two weeks later, Viktor was waiting impatiently on the side road outside Rostov when Georgy's Fiat pulled up in gathering darkness. The two young men emerged quickly from the cramped car to be met with warm embraces from Viktor, and after perfunctory greetings, the three of them moved behind the Fiat where Fedor untied the trunk lid and proudly showed the footlockers to the older man.

Viktor snapped one open, unwrapped the blankets, and nodded when he saw the heavy paper and wire bindings. It was as he remembered, and his nod was a signal. Georgy and Fedor never saw the man who came quietly out of the darkness and fired the quick two shots that splattered their brain tissue over the car's faded paint job. Their bodies slammed back off the car and pitched headlong into the snow.

The hitman's shots set off a chain of events. Viktor, who was a little afraid of his own hit man, immediately pulled his own Beretta and shot the assassin in the side of the head, spinning his body around and propelling it into the ditch beside the gravel road. As the assassin's body catapulted face-down into the snow, a woman bolted from the opposite side of the car.

8

In the dim light, Viktor had been focused on the meeting with Fedor, the hitman, and the contents of the trunk. The running woman started him. He snapped off a quick shot that went wide as the panicked girl made for the trees. He maneuvered around the car and tried again, but the running girl was already across the graveled road, and he missed again as she entered the nearby woods.

Cursing, he ran across the road and into the dark forest after her, but many years had gone by since Viktor had been a young man with a young man's stamina. As he labored through the brush, his breath came in gasps, and his chest was afire with pain. In the distance, he could hear the terrified girl's retreat as she crashed through the woods. But behind him was a public highway with three bodies, and more to the point, the two footlockers.

He fired a third futile shot in her general direction, then, cursing and wheezing, turned back toward the road where the two cars waited. No traffic passed in the fading light, and without interruption, he dragged the heavy footlockers from Fedor's Fiat to his larger Mercedes. Then with much effort, but still pumped on adrenalin, he stuffed the three bodies into the seats of Fedor's car, a grueling and bloody job that left him sweaty and panting.

After recovering his breath, he got into the driver's seat of the Fiat, turned the wheels toward the ravine below, slapped the manual shift lever into neutral, and released the brake. Returning to his own car, Viktor gently rested his front bumper against the Fiat's rear one and pushed it over the narrow shoulder of the road into the deep ravine. As gravity took hold, the old car bounced to the bottom of the gully, out of sight from the road. The blood and bits of bone beside the road would vanish beneath the snow.

As he drove away, Viktor's mind was not so much on the riches in the trunk of his car, but on the blonde woman who fled into the trees and whether he was going to have to find her and kill her. After some thought he decided against a further search. Who could she tell? If she went to the police in Rostov, he would find out and have her eliminated; more likely, she would just go away. In any case, he had a buyer for the packages in the trunk, and the best thing would be to make the sale quickly and then vanish to the West. He smiled as he drove back to Rostov.

~

In the forest, Valerlya crouched shivering in the snow. She knew he would leave, and she gambled he would go before she froze in the forest. As she pushed her way back through the trees, she thought about escape. But how? There was no safe place in Russia. But she was young and pretty; she had the money that Fedor and Georgy had given her to hold, and she was very bright—brighter than the men had credited She knew she had a secret, an awful secret, and it could get her killed.

TOP SECRET - DDO EYES ONLY

FROM STATION CHIEF KIEV

AM DEBRIEFING RUSSIAN NATIONAL WHO CLAIMS KNOWLEDGE OF THEFT OF FISSIONABLE MATERIEL PROBABLY HIGHLY ENRICHED URANIUM VICINITY PALASKOVA RF. SOURCE IS CIVILIAN FEMALE CLAIMING ASSASSINATION OF COMPANIONS. RELIABILITY JUDGED FAIR. QUANTITY OF MATERIEL ESTIMATED BY SOURCE VIC 100K.
DEBRIEF FOLLOWS.

TOP SECRET - DDO EYES ONLY

TO STATION CHIEF KIEV
FROM CIA LANGLEY

HIGHLY ENRICHED URANIUM THEFT ASSIGNED
CODEWORD RED AGATE.

TOP SECRET - RED AGATE EYES ONLY

Memo for: Secretary of State
              Secretary of Defense
              Dir Department of Energy
              Director CIA
              Asst to the president for National Security
              Affairs
              Cf: Dir of Operations, CIA
              Cf: Dep Dir Operations, CIA

This follows our discussion of 15 February. RED
AGATE has been discussed at highest levels and
Russian Federation has concurred with US
participation in joint survey. US will be permitted single
POC for survey team.
Request Director DOE nominate individual we have
discussed and get him to Moscow ASAP. POC CIA is
DDO. RF POC Moscow COL Egor Sokolov, FSB.

Restrict all communication to RED AGATE ONLY
access.

Steven R. McManus, Director of National Intelligence
Memorandum copy for the president

TOP SECRET - RED AGATE EYES ONLY

FOR DDO LANGLEY
FM STA CHIEF MOSCOW

FIELD REP CONFIRMS RED AGATE EST 144K HIGHLY
ENRICHED URANIUM BORON WRAPPING FULL
REPORT FOLLOWS.

Chapter 3

Late February - May

In midafternoon of a cold, gray day, a shabby coastal freighter pulled away from its slip on the south side of Rostov-on-Don, where the merchant ships tie up. The captain was a big Croatian with a bad complexion and an unlit black cigar clamped in his teeth. He was respected on the Rostov waterfront as an able seaman, but one who could be casual about who or what he took on board.

His crew was the usual Black Sea mix of Slavic nationalities, plus a few Filipinos and Chinese. The bulk cargo was scrap iron and low-cost manufactured goods, cheaper to send by sea—and this rusty old ship was the cheapest its customers could find. As the lines snaked aboard and the muddy water churned under the single propeller, the snow and ice piled on her deck gave the ratty, old ship a curious, spectral appearance.

This trip was a little out of the ordinary, even for this captain. At the last minute, the ship's owner had called and directed the Croatian to carry four passengers to Odessa and not to cast off until they were aboard. Just before the tide changed, four swarthy men arrived with little personal baggage and two old footlockers, brusquely declining assistance as they pulled and pushed them on hand trucks up the freighter's steep gangway and into one of the freighter's two passenger cabins.

The whole thing was odd, but these days, a man didn't ask questions. The passage was only two days—down the Sea of Azov, through the Kerchenska Gulf, then west. The captain shrugged, squinted at the balky radar, and then went to talk to the pilot as they worked down the channels through the treacherous Don marshes and out to sea.

~

As night fell two days later, the old tramp pulled into the Odessa docks not far from where the gleaming cruise ships tied up in the summer months.

The captain was busy with the routines of making port. The customs officer climbed the gangway, walked directly to the captain's cabin, pocketed his usual gift from the owners, and left, taking no note of the ship's passengers.

When a cell phone buzzed in their cabin, the four men gathered their backpacks, placed the footlockers on the hand trucks, and left as inconspicuously as they had arrived. From his place on the bridge, the captain saw them cross the deck and reach the gangway. Two men met them in the poor light at the pier, and they embraced. Then the footlockers were loaded into a nondescript van, and the men drove away, with the two following in a dark sedan.

The captain remotely wondered about the footlockers and the tall man who had greeted them at the foot of the gangway. He moved with authority, and even as the men had exchanged embraces, his posture remained aloof, almost regal. The captain shrugged and went back to the business of his ship.

Half an hour later in a nearby marina, a sleek, white, luxury yacht hauled her lines and put to sea.

~

As American intelligence began to focus on RED AGATE, a shipping company in Liberia put out feelers for a client to buy a Handy-class medium-displacement, break-bulk steamer of moderate draft of about 30,000 tons, a rate of advance of between fifteen and nineteen knots and geared with deck cranes for lifting cargo in and out of the ship. The vessel had to be capable of operating in ports without pier side cargo lifts. The Handy class was the most common class of cargo ships at sea, so the requirements and transaction were completely routine and unremarkable.

Within hours, a number of ships were on offer, and the Liberian executive purchased a relatively new Handy of medium size located not far from the client's desired homeport of Karachi.

Delivery details were worked out, and within days, the ship was at a dock just north of the Karachi shipyards. After a week, the ship moved to a small, more isolated yard and work began on modifications to her deck and power plant, alterations that involved substantial engine work and the replacement of the ship's propeller. The nature of the modifications caused some gossip around the yards, speculation that continued until a workman who had talked about the installation of heavy, steel, deck plating ended up floating face down in the oily water of the harbor with his throat slit from ear to ear. The talking stopped, but someone had taken notice.

TOP SECRET RED AGATE EYES ONLY

To: Dir, Defense Intelligence Agency, Washington D.C.
From: Defense Attache, USEMB Pakistan

Field reports indicate extensive modifications to Handy-class 30,000T freighter in Khawaja & Sons shipyard, KARACHI. Modifications reported by former crewman to be re-gearing engine and strengthened deck plating.

Purpose of modifications unknown but unlikely for commercial use. US Naval attaché attempted further survey but was turned away by armed security. According to contacts in port operations, subject ship is bunkering fuel and is clearing for MOGADISHU. Departure imminent.

TOP SECRET RED AGATE EYES ONLY

Memorandum for Director, National Intelligence
From Director, Naval Intelligence

Subject Handy-class freighter has not been located. Question whether subject ship actually shaped a course for MOGADISHU. USS TARPON (SSN–446) will continue search in patrol area.

16

Chapter 4

Mid-December

The tall man and his associate departed Karachi in the first-class cabin of Saudi Flight 334 to Madrid. Once there, they had a three-hour layover and boarded Air France Flight 1006 to Mexico City. The tall man didn't like flying, simply because it interrupted his daily ritual of prayer. He spent most of each flight sitting awake, considering the holy path of his work, and turning his plan over and over until satisfied that every eventuality had been covered. His companion snored loudly in the seat across the aisle.

When the Airbus 330-300 touched down at Benito Juarez International Airport seven hours later, both men passed easily through customs into the reception area, where they were met by a driver and security detail. With only carry-on bags, they left the airport quickly and drove away on the 602.

A short time later, they turned right into the San Bernardino suburbs, where a Bell helicopter awaited them, rotors turning. After a thirty-minute flight to the east, they landed on a private airstrip just outside the small town of Cuamautzingo and transferred again, this time to a Lear 40XR executive jet. They immediately lifted off for the long northeast flight to Cuauhtema, where they settled into the guesthouse in the *Jefe's* compound overlooking Lake Bustillos.

FM DDO LANGLEY VA
TO SECSTATE
  SECDEF
  DNI
  DIR DPT OF ENERGY
  DIR CIA
  DIR FBI
    Cf: DIR DEA

DIR DEA REPORTS MEETING VICINITY CUAUHTEMA MEXICO BETWEEN MAX ABARZO ZETA CARTEL AND ARABIC PAIR LED BY MAN TENTATIVELY IDENTIFIED AS ABU HUSAM AL DIN. PURPOSE WAS TO GAIN ZETA ASSISTANCE IN STRIKE AT US MAINLAND. PRESENT WAS FELIX GUZMANN FORMERLY HEAD OF ZETA OPS IN MONTEREY. ZETA CONTRIBUTION APPARENTLY TO PROVIDE FAST BOAT TO UNKNOWN LOCATION BY DATE NOT SPECIFIED. SOURCE HAS PREVIOUSLY BEEN RELIABLE AND HAS BEEN EVACUATED FOR SAFETY AND FURTHER DEBRIEF.

~

Snow fell on northern Virginia, and from his tenth-floor office at Langley, the CIA Deputy Director for Operations Ralph Ward could just make out the Potomac River a few miles away through the gray twilight. The DDO was a gray man himself, older than the director of operations and certainly older than the politically-appointed CIA director. Ward was a professional whose experience in covert operations went back decades. He was up for retirement, but his boss had asked him to stay on a little longer, and for the sake of their old friendship, he had agreed.

A single sheet of paper rested on his desk under his fingertips. His eyes followed the falling snow without seeing. When the knock came on his door, he stirred, and his secretary showed in his visitor.

"Hello, Sal," Ward said.

Sal Leoni only nodded. Ward felt the radiation of the man's contained energy.

"You read in on RED AGATE?" the DDO asked.

"Yes, sir," the short man answered, still standing. There were no other chairs in the office other than the one Ward sat in.

"What have you got Dugan doing?"

"He's been in Pakistan," Sal answered. "Yesterday I told him to come home."

The DDO smiled. "Reading my mind again?"

Sal did not smile. "He might be useful."

Chapter 5

January

The Atlantic Ocean is an empty place, even at longitude 13 degrees, 25 minutes, in line with the approaches to the English Channel. The weather was foul, normal for this time of year. Winter in the Atlantic was not for the casual traveler, but bad weather was actually part of the plan begun many years before, when this opportunity had been foreseen.

The Handy-class freighter had shed several identities in ports around the Indian Ocean and Southwestern Pacific on its way to Jakarta as part of the stream of normal commercial shipping. Now it was on its fifth identity as a jack-of-all-trades steamer with a load of chemicals and pet food, products of Pakistan, through Suez and bound for Liverpool.

Mid-ocean, she passed near an almost identical ship bound for Baltimore, with almost identical cargo. The two vessels briefly hove-to while ships' papers were exchanged with the use of a rubberized launch. The second ship, now wearing the Handy's identity, reversed its course toward England as the first turned west toward America. The weather began to deteriorate, a sign of blessing for their mission.

~

Even in the mid-Atlantic, the Handy had no trouble rendezvousing a day later with the white yacht, although the transfer of cargo was difficult in the dirty weather and heaving seaway. The two vessels came alongside with bumpers and fenders deployed, but they still scraped and banged together while the larger ship's cargo cranes were used to transfer a dozen large crates and a pallet with two oblong shipping containers from the yacht into the Handy's five large cargo holds.

After the transfer, the yacht stood away from the freighter. Its tender, pitching and rolling in seas that burst over its bow, ferried the tall man and one of the yacht's crew to the Handy. As soon as they had gone up the heaving accommodation ladder, the tossing tender returned to the yacht. The white ship immediately turned away at speed, lest the American satellites detect the rendezvous. They had eyes that could even see through clouds.

As the merchantman turned westward, the tall man and the ship's captain conferred. The Arabs have long seafaring traditions, and there were many Arabic seamen who were willing to take the road of jihad. With the exception of the few uncomprehending Mexicans who had come aboard in Aden to represent their *Jefe's* interests, the crew was now entirely dedicated to the mission. The jihad had been long in planning, waiting for the day when someone would appear with highly-enriched uranium. When Viktor came into the international black market with the materiel, the tall man and his team were ready. Now Viktor was in an unmarked grave, the bombs had been built in a weapons shop near Karachi, and the ship was prepared for the mission.

Now all that remained was to negotiate the Americans' security measures and rendezvous with their destiny.

~

The Handy steamed westward at 19 knots. Her modified engines and special prop consumed fuel extravagantly. She was capable of higher speeds, but to avoid notice, she stayed within the upper-average rate of advance for her class as she pounded through the empty sea.

As she steamed in the empty Atlantic, the ship vibrated with the sound of riveting and welding. The large crates that came aboard in mid-ocean were opened, and their contents mounted at appropriate places around the ship, and then concealed under superstructure and cargo containers. Several new antennae joined the usual cluster of domes and long whips atop the superstructure.

While the weapons were being installed, the tall man spent his time in prayer, in discussions with his family's long-serving imam, and in inspecting the ship's peculiar cargo. At his direction, the ship's crew transferred a portion of the ship's legitimate cargo to the holds near the two coffin-shaped metal shipping containers. Other cargo was stacked around them, using the ship's cranes. When the work was completed there was no sign of the hidden cargo.

~

By direction of the president:

The RED AGATE interagency working group is convened at CIA Langley.

CIA will continue as lead agency, RED AGATE.

Assistant to the president for National Security Affairs, Dr. Harvey Winstead, is appointed Director of RED AGATE working group with appropriate authority.

Point of contact for this action is the Chief of Staff to the president.

s/ John Forester
Chief of Staff

Chapter 6

Late January

As the Handy made its way across the wintry Atlantic, the United States and the Mexican government focused electronic collection on the *Jefe's* compound at Cuauhtema. *El Jefe* and his henchmen were not nearly so scrupulous at protecting their electronic conversations as were the Arabs, an oversight on the tall man's part.

With little effort, National Security Agency's eavesdroppers traced calls along the Zeta network from Cuauhtema to Atlanta, Georgia, and from there to a Zeta cell in the Miami area. Within twenty-four hours, DEA agents, acting in support of a highly compartmented request for help from the FBI and the Langley working group, followed three members of the cell to a small yacht brokerage on the north side of Fort Lauderdale.

~

FM DIR DEA
TO RED AGATE WORKING GROUP/WINSTEAD

AGENT MIAMI REPORTS TWO INDIVIDUALS ARRIVED YESTERDAY FROM MEXICO CITY MOVING TO PURCHASE GO-FAST FROM DEALER KNOWN TO WORK WITH CARTELS. AGENT WILL INSTALL TRACKING DEVICE ON GO-FAST. FURTHER DETAILS AS WE HAVE THEM.

GUZMANN AND ASSOCIATES WHEREABOUTS UNKNOWN.

Chapter 7

Friday in Late January

Once he left the *Jefe's* hacienda, Felix Guzmann did not use a cell phone again and thus slipped beneath the dragnets of the U.S. and Mexico. He and two other members of the *Jefe's* personal staff drove to the airport in Monterrey where they boarded an American airlines flight to Dulles. On arrival, they passed through U.S. Customs with Mexican passports and Border Crossing Cards, made three calls on disposable cell phones that they immediately discarded, rented a car under an assumed name, and drove to Baltimore to begin their part of the American phase.

Five members of a Ukrainian mafia that dominated crime in the Baltimore suburbs met Guzmann at an address in the city.

Within hours, a convoy of five dark SUVs left Baltimore and headed south, down interstate 97, then to Maryland route 3, and finally onto U.S. highway 301. They crossed the Potomac River on the 301 bridge and stopped for the night at a motel on the Virginia side.

On Saturday morning, they breakfasted in a local restaurant, loaded their cars, and entered highway 301 to the left, and began to follow small coastal roads down the northern neck. Three other SUVs later left the city and followed them down, bringing even more muscle for the occupation. Their objective was the small fishing village of Brewer, on the mouth of the Potomac River.

~

At the Admiral's Arms, Brewer's best and only bed and breakfast inn, Cassandra Riley expected a guest that Saturday morning. The season was over; in fact, the weather forecast was bad, but the voice on the phone had been cultured and persuasive. He said he was interested in land around Brewer and was taking a weekend to check it out. He would stay at her B&B for a day or two only.

Cassandra needed the business, so she was looking forward to the company. Six-year-old Erin helped, as she always did, and asked chatty questions about their visitor until the dark car pulled up. Cassandra instinctively checked her makeup in the living room mirror, patted her hair into place, then noticed there were several men in the car, not just one. And then another car drove up.

~

An hour later, the leader was satisfied. The building offered a good view of the town and the bay beyond. The high ground would assist communications, and his technicians were already setting up their equipment on the second floor. The brat was out of the way, held by his men in the SUV. The others were rounding up the citizens of the pitiful little town, and the child would be taken to be with the other hostages. It gave him leverage with the mother.

He looked appraisingly at the frightened woman. He noted her attractive, pale face, her auburn hair, and the way her rounded breasts strained against the pinioning of her arms. Perhaps there would be some pleasure in this job after all.

"*Senora*, we will be your guests. You will cook, and if you do precisely—precisely—what we ask, all will be well," he said with a smile.

The technicians went about their tasks mechanically. Their assignments were important but not complicated. Installing the satellite phone was simple and only required plugging the charging cradle into the wall. The handset charged in the cradle and operated like any telephone. Satellite calls were difficult to intercept, and the phone would only be used for shore-to-ship calls to arrange the rendezvous.

The suitcase instrument that let them intercept and track cell phone signals was also pulled from the second SUV and put into operation. It was passive and emitted no electronic signature that could be traced. Likewise, the motion-sensor setup emitted no signals. A man quickly installed the monitor and then left for the forest to install the cameras and sensors to give security in the woods around the house.

The limited-area cell tower was a constant emitter though, and it had to be tested to supplement the weak and intermittent commercial signals that reached Brewer. The town's electronic isolation was important for the Zeta's plans. They needed a reliable, local system to coordinate their operations, and their experts had assured the leader that the low-power signal would be undetectable, based on their previous experience in rural Mexico.

~

But even the low-power signal erupted like an exploding skyrocket into an electromagnetic environment already under heavy scrutiny as the best intelligence operators in the United States government searched for ways to connect the various clues that had been dropping at their feet in the previous weeks.

The supersensitive ears on the patrolling AWACS, the antennas on the satellites and on the high-flying drones all alerted on the cell tower. The rough cellphone conversations that followed the takeover of the town were recorded and analyzed. Discarded cellphones or not, the Zetas' signals discipline was beyond poor.

Had the Arabs known, they would have aborted the mission. But they did not know, any more than they knew about the search for the Handy that had been underway for months.

Chapter 8

Saturday 1700

Harvey Winstead, the president's national security advisor, was the man on the spot. When the search for the enriched uranium began to focus on a renegade ship and the Zetas, Winstead advised the president that the active phase of RED AGATE should continue to be run from Langley, despite opposition from the Pentagon, the FBI, and various legislation that restricted the agency's operations inside the United States. It made no practical sense, Winstead argued, to uproot a successful team at this critical point. Workarounds could be found.

The president concurred, and to Winstead's surprise, tasked him to coordinate and direct the multi-agency search, reporting directly to the White House —to the president personally—with the CIA as lead agency. By mid-January, Winstead visited the planning team daily, masking his trips from the press and even from his own staff.

Not a physically imposing man, Winstead sometimes gave an impression of academic distraction that hid a first-class mind. The professional spies, lawmen, and military officers whose bureaucratic noses were out of joint, and who initially dismissed him as a "professor," learned quickly that he ran a taut ship. After a few embarrassing episodes, they settled into what had become a smoothly running team.

Now, on a late Wednesday afternoon, the professor got unwelcome news.

"Shit," he said. "How sure are we?"

"We have the intercepts," the NSA representative said. "That's what they say." He spoke for the collective electronic intercept community. Since the Snowden revelations, NSA had been wary of domestic surveillance, but Winstead demanded that NSA speak for the entire electronic intelligence community. Other representatives in the room nodded. They could confirm NSA's findings with their own.

"How many?"

"We think about a hundred."

Winstead turned to the CIA representative. As he did with the intelligence community, the national security advisor demanded CIA speak for the operators. FBI was unhappy, and its director had gone over Winstead's head to the president, but CIA kept the lead. "What's going on, Ralph?"

The CIA's deputy director for operations, Ralph Ward, cleared his throat. "We think the Zetas are giving themselves some space, since the ship's arrival time is uncertain. They're making sure they can base their go-fast without interference. We aren't absolutely positive, of course, but I'm pretty sure that's the game."

"Right under our noses," Winstead said. "What happens to the hostages when this is over?"

The DEA representative and the DDO exchanged glances. Then the DDO said, "They kill them." There was a momentary silence.

"Kill a hundred people?" Winstead was incredulous. "Kill them all? Kids, women, the works?"

The DDO nodded toward a thickset man who cleared his throat. "These are Zetas," the DEA representative said. "They are the most ruthless cartel in the Western Hemisphere and kill without compunction. They've killed before—women and kids. They'd kill thousands for enough money. A hundred people dead won't matter to them, and anyway, they figure that if the Arabs get the bombs through, nobody will care about a hundred people down in Virginia. So they get away in the confusion."

"Shit," Winstead said again. "What's the plan?"

The room went silent. After a heartbeat, the DDO spoke up again. "We have an idea," he said. "Not everybody likes it."

The FBI representative turned red in the face, and despite the tension, Winstead saw a ghost of a smile cross the military officers' faces.

"You know Sal Leoni," the DDO said. "Sal's been to see you before."

Winstead took in the short man with thinning hair in the back of the room, nodding an acknowledgment. "Go on," he said to the DDO.

"We," the DDO's glance took in the men and women in the room, "have already begun to build the intelligence for what I'm about to propose, and Sal has the people ready. The man, really."

Chapter 9

Sunday 0900

The White House situation room was actually a series of rooms, physically and electronically one of the most secure places in Washington, D.C. There was space for the technicians and experts at the fingertips of the president of the United States in any crisis, and the makeup of the staff changed with whatever crisis confronted the United States.

But the inner sanctum where the president makes decisions that could rock the globe is surprisingly modest. It could be mistaken for any conference room anywhere in corporate America; its very sparseness reinforcing in subtle ways the power concentrated there in times of crisis.

A long table ran the length of the room, surrounded by a series of black upholstered chairs, one with a back slightly higher than the others, with a discrete presidential seal impressed on the leather. On this occasion it was occupied. Other chairs and small tables were spotted unobtrusively around the walls. On the long wall facing the high-backed chair was a large, flat video screen that supported either presentations or video teleconferencing. There was no other ornamentation.

Now, the seats around the president were filled with principals or principal deputies, and at the opposite wall, standing just to the left of the screen, Winstead briefed the group. The chairman of the Joint Chiefs sat next to the president, and the directors of the Central Intelligence Agency, the Federal Bureau of Investigation, and the National Security Agency were in their chairs at the table. Further down sat the director of Homeland Security, the only woman present. The vice president was on a speaking tour and was being briefed remotely. He would not return during the crisis.

"What do we know?" the president asked abruptly. His calendar was, as always, crowded, and a visit by the German prime minister had been delayed.

Winstead looked at his notes. *He's pissed,* he thought. "This information is raw, but it's all we have. We know that one of three ships coming toward the United States is probably carrying one, and possibly two, nuclear devices. We've been tracking the modification of the ship for a year—"

"How big?" the president interrupted. He meant the bombs, Winstead knew. The president knew the details almost by heart, but as always, he wanted it all, every time.

Winstead looked at the director of the CIA, allowing him to answer the question.

"About ten kilotons apiece," the director said, "given the amount of nuclear materiel stolen. Almost the same size of the Hiroshima bomb, each."

The president looked at him for a level moment, then turned back to Winstead.

The national security advisor spoke. "We know that the Islamic Jihadist Front, an independent splinter group largely financed by Saudi money, made an alliance about a month ago with the Zetas—the bloodiest of the Mexican drug cartels—to help the IJF use the bombs to attack two American cities. We are fairly sure that the IJF owns and operates the ship that's carrying the bombs,

34

though we have not been able to establish exact ownership." *That's for later*, he thought.

Winstead turned to the video screen, where a map of the U.S. east coast appeared with a red line tracing from Florida to the Chesapeake Bay. "We know that a Zeta operative recently bought a go-fast boat in the Miami-Fort Lauderdale area and is bringing it up the east coast toward the target area. We believe that a member of the IJF is aboard. We think–*think*–the go-fast will be a delivery vehicle for one of the bombs."

Winstead had worked for the president for years, in and out of the think-tanks, through two campaigns, and now the White House, and he knew the president preferred facts to speculation. But he gave him some speculation now, since it was all they really had.

"We believe that the intent of the operation is for the ship to rendezvous with the go-fast, and then one or both will detonate nuclear devices in the waterfront of a major American city, maybe two." He glanced around the room. The intelligence chiefs and the chairman of the Joint Chiefs of Staff nodded agreement. "Almost certainly one of those cities will be Washington, the other probably Baltimore."

The president stirred in his chair, a sign of impatience. He knew all this, and he raised his hand to cut Winstead off.

"There's nothing new here," he said. "When we met two days ago, I approved plans to stop all ships approaching our outer security zones, apprehending their crews and escorting them to a neutral port," the president said. "We agreed that we can deal with the Zetas after the principal threat has been eliminated. I thought all this was settled." He looked at Winstead and at the body language around the room. "Well?"

"There has been a complication," Winstead said carefully. He explained the situation in concise terms. "We think the Zetas are holding over a hundred hostages near here, in a remote town on the bay," he said. He touched the display where the Potomac met the bay. The map immediately changed to a gray-black satellite photograph of a few scattered buildings on a waterfront.

Winstead went on. "This gives them a secure base from which to launch the go-fast, which at this moment is in route and close to the town. We are reasonably sure that if we take the ship at sea, the reaction on shore will be to kill all the hostages to cover the Zetas' tracks." He took a deep breath. "We recommend holding off until we can free the hostages."

There was a silence. The president looked levelly at Winstead, then at the overhead picture on the screen. Winstead could see the anger roiling inside him. The president fought for, then gained, controlled of his emotions. He waited a heartbeat, looking around the room. The people around the table met his eyes. He turned back to the bespectacled man at the screen.

"So you're telling me we have to let this thing get closer?" he asked. "Am I hearing you recommend that we let terrorists bring nuclear weapons into U.S. waters?"

"Mister President," Winstead said evenly, "of course the decision is yours. We are pointing out that the immediate seizure of the three vessels that fit the profile of the terrorists' ship will probably lead to the deaths of over a hundred people. We are not saying that we should let the ship penetrate to its likely targets."

Taking a deep breath, he went on. "We're saying that we don't have to move now. There are important things we don't know. We don't know which ship of the three is our target, and we don't know where the hostages are being held, except in the town. We don't know what kind of constraints are on them, though we are in agreement that they are in imminent peril. We still have some time to work out the answers."

The president looked carefully at his national security advisor. Winstead returned the president's look, then said, "There is an alternative plan that has been proposed. It will require a presidential decision and cooperation between the federal agencies represented

36

in this room." His gaze seemed to linger on the director of the FBI. "There is some risk, but we believe it has a good chance of success, and there are backups." He did not have to mention that the people around the table were in agreement. At this level, agreement was taken for granted.

FBI still doesn't like it, Winstead thought. *Screw him. I'll find some way to give him some credit and appease him.*

The president nodded.

Winstead motioned with his hand and a thickset, balding man in an off-the-rack suit walked to the front of the room and faced the president. His big arms hung loosely at his side, and he gave the impression of calm, contained energy.

"Mister President," Winstead said. "This is Sal Leoni. He is director of covert operations in the CIA's operations directorate. He can explain the concept better than I."

The president made a *go on* gesture with his fingers, and Sal began to speak without notes or slides. His voice had the gravity of a man used to giving orders.

"Mister President," he said. "We have a plan we think will work and still guarantee the security of our cities. It gives us a very good chance of recovering the hostages." As he spoke, the president leaned forward, and the room became absolutely silent, save for Sal's voice.

He spoke for five minutes. When he finished, the president leaned back, silent for a full thirty seconds, looking at Sal while he turned the decision over in his mind. No one thought of speaking. The dialogue was between the president of the United States and the little man in the ill-fitting suit.

"This depends on doing a lot in a very short time," the president said.

"Yes, sir, it does."

"And you want to send only one man."

"Yes, sir. One man is less liable to be detected than two or more." One of the generals stirred but kept silent. "We don't know for sure where the hostages are," Sal continued. "We think there are two locations, but there may be more. In any case, the prisoners are probably side-by-side with unstable, ruthless murderers. The slightest thing can set these people off on a killing spree. One man halves the chances of being detected and increases the chance of bringing the hostages out alive."

"You must be confident in your man."

"Yes, sir, I am. He's the best."

Chapter 10

Tuesday 2100

Neil Dugan relaxed in the water, pushing gently with his fins and breathing easily through the snorkel. From shore, the wetsuit was invisible in the darkness and the waves. Even at closer range, Dugan's torso appeared to be a half-submerged log, rolling and tossing in the northeast chop. He was still thirty yards offshore when his gloved hands brushed along the oozy bottom, and though he expected it, the contact sent shivers up his arm.

He paused there, balanced on his fingertips, looking for the landmarks that the overheads said would be there. It wasn't easy. The low, thick clouds of the approaching storm blocked out any starlight, and the water washing over his mask blurred his vision. There were no lights on shore. For long minutes he hung in the cold water, peering through the streaked lenses of his mask, rising and falling naturally in the waves that were washing him gently toward shore.

Dugan took his time. He was a big, cautious man, a little old for this kind of fieldwork, and beginning to hear complaints from his body. Being careful kept him alive, and he was careful now. After scanning the land for signs of movement, he began to move toward the shore, blending with the pattern of the incoming waves.

While his body was held just below the surface by the weight belt, he hand-walked along the bottom, away from the dark loom of what he believed to be the boathouse on his left. He lost his grip on the bottom when an especially strong wave nearly rolled him over, but as he moved closer to shore, his fingers sank deeper into the ooze, and he gained more control.

After another five minutes, he was sure he'd found the correct place. The distant, dark bulk of the boathouse was on his left, and a stretch of sandy beach glowed white before him. Moving carefully to avoid disturbing the patterns of the wavelets washing against the shore, he pushed backwards against the incoming tide while he continued to hand-walk to the right toward the marsh, still rolling with the incoming waves but now occasionally touching the muddy bottom with his chest as the water washed over him. After more minutes of slow movement, his eyes constantly probing the dark shore, he reached the tall grasses that grew out of the marsh into the salty water.

Still there was no reaction from the land, though he caught a glimmer of light in the direction of the big house, farther from the water. Once he reached the reeds, he relaxed and let the tide wash him in, slowly moving like an enormous black salamander through the grasses and the muck that had gathered at the water's edge. With only his black-hooded head, the snorkel, and mask above water, Dugan reached the indistinct line of solid ground along the edge of the marshy shore and lay in the detritus of old leaves and tangled branches for another ten minutes. His senses were stretched for the slightest sound, the merest hint of movement. Nothing.

With infinite care, still lying in the muck and with his eyes probing the darkness ahead, he eased his hands down to slip off the fins and gloves, thrusting them back in the water. The weight belt, snorkel, and mask followed. He unsnapped a small waterproof bag from a waist belt and took out the sneakers and the night vision goggles. No gun, no radio—the one was futile against these odds, the other dangerous against men with electronic countermeasures. A leg sheath held his knife, and the microchip embedded in Dugan's hood let the overhead sensors follow his progress.

Without looking away from the shore, he pulled on the stretchy sneakers and slipped the NVG harness over his hood. He took a final look around the shore and forest before dropping the eyepiece in front of one eye. He nodded to himself and slowly began to crawl forward, heading for the greater darkness under the tall pines at the water's edge. The stalk had begun.

Hunters know that hearing is often the most enhanced of the senses at night. Even allowing for the rising wind, the rustle of the reeds, and the creaking of trees, Dugan counted on his ears to warn him of danger before his eyes would, even with the NVG.

The one-eyed goggle lit up the world around him in a green glow, exposing the woods in front and the darker shadows cast by the trees. With the goggle set on ambient collection, he scanned the darkness, moving his head slowly from left to right, then back again. There was no sign of infrared lights and no glint of other passive collectors.

Dugan crawled through the tangle of old branches and into deeper darkness under the pines along the shore. With great care, he brought his knees up, then raised himself to a squat, and in five minutes he was into the trees, moving slowly, pausing every five steps to listen with an intensity that pained his ears. Still nothing. Crouching, he began to move on an angle toward the big house that rose up before him in the darkness.

~

High above the seacoast, above the weather, so high that the earth's curvature would have been visible had there been human eyes on board, the dark gray RQ-4 Global Hawk banked gently in its long orbit over the boatyard and the house. Along the drone's fuselage, sensitive antenna listened for coded whispers, and a rotating turret near the nose fixed its unblinking eye on the tiny chip in Dugan's wetsuit.

Other sensors followed the deployment of the four SEAL delivery boats from their base near Norfolk to waiting positions further up the bay, and still others tracked the location and speed of the three civilian cargo ships in the deeper waters off the coast. One of the critical tasks for the hastily organized operations center at Langley Air Force Base on the Virginia peninsula was to single out the target ship. Each of the three ships passed intensive security checks at their ports of origin, but the Handy's mid-ocean rendezvous had not been detected. Coast Guard security teams had boarded each vessel earlier, and each had been permitted—on last-minute orders from the highest levels—to proceed through the coastal identification zone.

At CIA headquarters and at Langley Air Force Base, planners and agents fanned out with their critical tasks. At the Air Force base, pilots manned the controls of the unmanned aerial vehicles in their high-altitude orbits, feeding their information into the operations center and the White House situation room. With presidential approval, the operation threw itself together, tasking assets and gathering people on the fly, often by word of mouth alone, since there were so many moving parts and not much time. Throughout other parts of the government that dealt in classified operations, there was a sense that something big was happening, but no word leaked. There was no time for leaks.

Sal Leoni stood in the operations room in front of the video screen like the ringmaster in a circus, balding and rumpled, in his shirtsleeves, cuffs rolled back, and fists on his hips. Standing next to a man in the uniform of an Air Force lieutenant general, Sal looked over the big screen at the drone feed and the data streaming in from the Global Hawk and other sensors deployed around the coast. There was a quiet, disciplined hum from the specialists manning the workstations. Most of the staff was in Air Force blue.

To speed things up, Sal and his three-star deputy had simply taken over the operations staff at Langley. Sal then added a rear admiral and some naval officers, recruited from the Naval Station Norfolk, to oversee the Navy's part in the plan, as well as a few civilians.

But there was no question who was in charge. At a glance, Sal looked like a short, slightly disreputable used car salesman standing next to the six-foot, trim Air Force general, but he radiated authority. This was his operation, and he had a direct line to the national command center and the White House situation room that only he was authorized to use.

All the painstaking global intelligence collection, the analysis, the educated guesses, and a number of murdered or missing agents boiled down to this quiet room and the orbiting drones. Sal focused on the intermittent white dot representing Neil Dugan moving through the shoreline brush toward the dark trees. An officer approached the general, handed him a sheet of paper, and spoke to him in low tones. The general turned to Sal.

"Sal, the forecast is shittier and shittier," he said, too lightly.

Sal turned his head. His black Sicilian eyes glittered for a moment, and the general had a momentary glimpse of why Sal had become a legend in the CIA's operations directorate.

"How shitty is *shitty*, Rick?" he asked evenly.

The general's lips narrowed, and Sal knew he had gotten his point across. This was no time to be flippant.

The general gathered his thoughts and answered with more care. "The front is moving down the coast faster than we'd forecasted. Bottom line is a gale from the northeast, starting in two or three hours. Low ceilings, heavy rain becoming sleet, temps in the low thirties, ice. Worst of all, winds in excess of thirty knots. A real nor'easter.

"It won't affect the high-fliers, but the medium and especially low-altitude birds are probably going to be blown off station or iced out. And that means comms with your man in the field may get spotty."

They had figured the weather would get bad, but this was building up to be worse than they'd planned. A line flitted through Sal's mind from long ago: bad weather favors the attacker. *So who is the attacker now?* He shrugged it off and turned back to watch the little white dot creep through the trees, winking on and off as limbs and branches broke the signal to the drone. *As always, the weather gets a vote,* he thought.

He looked at the general and imperceptibly shrugged. A ghost of a smile touched his lips as he remembered the first time he had met Neil Dugan. "Well," he said to the airman, "he's in. And he was an infantryman. Special Forces. A little rain won't slow him down."

After a minute, the general smiled, feeling the beginnings of friendship for this short man with the laundry-bag shirt. Sal already had his respect.

Chapter 11

Wednesday 0100

Dugan took a knee in the trees, far enough back for concealment, but with a good view through the NVG at the old white house on the knoll. At one time, it was imposing, multistoried and high roofed, with the wide, sweeping porches common in the south before air conditioning. The intelligence said the builder was a country lawyer named Walker who was later a state senator, with interests in the oyster packing house and some local farmland. When he passed on and the next two generations spent his money, the house went quietly to rental, and then finally to a caretaker.

Now it sat alone and shabby, in the company of a few rundown outbuildings and sheds, on its little peninsula in the bay. Some of the shades on the ground floor windows were drawn and dark, but others were bright and showed figures inside. There was no light in the upper floors at all.

He waited a minute more, then moved slowly and smoothly across the open space between the trees and the house, where decades ago children had played on the lawn. From years of experience, Dugan knew the special skill of moving at night, blending silently and without apparent effort with the normal noises and movements of the dark. The trees and shrubs that tossed in the increasing wind covered his movement.

He had just made it across the open space when the sounds of the approaching storm were abruptly interrupted by male laughter from the house. Then a voice, too indistinguishable to understand, burst from one of the windows. A door banged open, and the dark shape of a man walked out on the porch to Dugan's right.

The agent froze, then slowly began to sink behind one of the cars on line between his position and the house, the dull black of his wetsuit blending into the shadows. The man from the house spat, scratched, called something to someone inside, and then walked away in the darkness toward the boathouse on Dugan's left. The language had not been English.

Dugan held his position for a long minute while he considered the words he'd heard. *Not Spanish,* he thought. *Eastern European, maybe Romanian or Ukrainian. We didn't expect this. Sal won't like being surprised.*

For some heartbeats he held his position, unmoving, and then he began easing slowly around the car and toward the house, avoiding the pools of light cast by the windows. As he moved nearer, he pushed the optics back on his head, trusting more to his eyes as he got closer to the target. As he slipped slowly through the darkness, rough voices inside the house began to be distinct over the sounds of the wind, and now Spanish was discernable, more by the cadence and phrasing than by individual words.

He found a line of low shrubs and sheltered behind them, pressed against the wall and under one of the unshaded windows. *Sounds like we have a little United Nations inside. Probably picked up some hired help in northern Virginia or Baltimore. Lots of that going around up there.*

The back porch door opened again, a few feet to his right, and another figure came down the steps, moving briskly but not running. Not alarmed. Dugan crouched behind the shrubs while the figure passed, headed away to the left. After a minute, a car started in the pines, and Dugan had just enough time to ease to the ground behind the foliage before the car's lights swept the wall behind him in a bright glow.

The car pulled up next to the house and doors slammed. More voices. And then the car moved away, turning from the house to the driveway that ran down an avenue of pines, and Dugan was again in darkness, watching the retreating taillights.

But he was not alone. Two men remained where the car had been, their dark shadows blending into the night, their voices unhurried and casual. A flare of a match briefly lit a brutal face and then receded in the glow of a cigarette. Dugan waited with the patience of long experience. Finally, as a spattering rain began, the two men finished their conversation and headed back to the porch, passing within feet of where Dugan knelt in the brush, his hand on the hilt of his ankle knife.

The rain spit drops that warned of more to come. The wind picked up—the advance echelon of the storm that Dugan and Sal had seen—and the temperature dropped. Inactivity made the wetsuit uncomfortable, but the suit's dull black perfectly suited his needs. With the waterproof face paint, Dugan was as invisible in the night as a black cat. *And twice as skittish,* he thought. *Used up all my nine lives. And this crowd is more interesting than just a bunch of Latino thugs.* Easing forward, he flattened along the side of the house, estimating his position in relation to the brightly lit window.

As he focused on getting closer, a part of his mind analyzed and classified the men he stalked. *No guards,* he thought. *Everybody inside on a cold night. Big guys, tough guys, Russians or southern European along with the Latinos, maybe Ukrainian mafia but amateurish.* If the loud men were in *this* room, Dugan decided, then his business was elsewhere.

It was early yet, not even midnight. Creeping cautiously under the bright window, he worked his way slowly around the house, pausing every few feet to give his straining ears a chance to *really* hear the noises of the night. The rain fell harder, making concealment easier but also muting the house-sounds he needed to orient his movement. Finally, on the other side of the sprawling old mansion, he found a darkened window that seemed about right for his purpose. It lifted silently to his touch and he pushed gently upward, hearing the ancient sash weights falling inside the frame and waiting for the squeak of the rollers. When it came, he stopped for a long minute. No reaction. He started to lift again and finally the opening was man-size.

In a second, Dugan was through the window and into the room, knife in one hand, the other reaching out in the darkness. No ambient light here. Nothing. He flipped down the night vision goggle, switched on the battery-powered infrared, and in the green glow, saw piles of bedding and boxes. Junk of one kind or another littered the floor, and a false step would have brought him down.

In the corner was another door, and he suspected, stairs beyond. He took one slow step into the room toward the door, then another. But before he could move again, loud voices approached from the other side, and he had just enough time to drop behind a pile of bedding, turn off the goggle and flip it up before the door opened and light spilled in. An older man, unshaven and in a soiled shirt, was shoved roughly into the room.

"Here!" an accented voice said from the door. "Get your stinking blanket."

An older, grizzled man with great sorrow on his shoulders shambled into the dim room toward the opposite side. His captor watched from the doorway. As the old man bent to pick up the blanket, he turned away from the watcher at the door, and his eyes met Dugan's. He hesitated. He saw a dark figure, glistening slightly in the dimness, a black face, white eyes. A knife. And Dugan's finger on his lips, with all the electric urgency he could muster. For a split-second, time was frozen. Then the old man's eyes narrowed, he nodded minutely, picked up a blanket, turned tiredly away with his prize, and went back through the door. It closed. There was the sound of a blow, a loud laugh, and footsteps.

Dugan's fingers gripped the hilt of the knife so hard they hurt, but now was not the time. It was time to go. *They're here,* he thought. *Solved that piece.*

He brought the eyepiece down and switched on the infrared, crossing the room and slipping out the window in one motion. The rain fell hard now, washing out his night vision but making it unlikely that the men inside the house would be coming out for a casual look around.

That's the problem with second-rate talent, he thought. *They like to stay warm and dry. Not a bad idea, actually.* Dugan turned, silently lowered the window behind him, flipped the eyepiece back up, and knelt behind the hedge to let his eyes adjust to the darkness. The rain made seeing harder, but it also deadened sound, so moving could be quicker and the route back to the water could be more direct. It was colder. The black wetsuit kept him from freezing on a night that was fast turning out to be miserable, but the cold seeped through.

God pity sailors on a night like this, he thought, even as he crossed the yard and threaded his way among the trees back to the fins and snorkel.

Dugan was just crossing through the blackness under the trees when his foot struck a soft object, and a deep shadow rose almost under his feet with a mumbled question. For a split-second, the agent froze. The sleepy and confused guard in a hooded rain jacket struggled to sort out who had kicked him awake in the storm. The man's neck was exposed to Dugan's blade, but instead the agent tore himself away, running for the water as the confused Zeta hesitated, then began to shout in Spanish as he pulled out a 9mm pistol.

Dugan dashed through the pines toward the beach, and the pistol popped ineffectively behind him. *You'd be better off just throwing it at me,* he thought as he dashed toward the water.

But the man's shouts got better results, and the lights were coming on in the house as Dugan reached the marsh. Somebody fired a submachine gun that exploded somewhere behind him. Pausing for a split-second, Dugan shoved the knife back into its leg holder, ripped the night vision harness off his head and threw it into the deeper water offshore and groped for his facemask. Then he double-timed into the surf, and without looking for the rest of his equipment, he crammed the mask over his face while he ran toward deeper water.

The same squidgy bottom that was so helpful coming in was now a potential deathtrap, sucking at his ankles. Deep water was a long way off, but the lashing rain and wind came in harder and masked the sounds of his flight, as behind him, lights came on and flashlight beams began to play across the water to his right.

His legs churned the slush, and his breath was hoarse in his ears as he ran in knee-deep ooze. The lights continued to play along the shoreline. He cut left and finally made it to waist-high water, flopped belly-first into the choppy surf, pushing his body down without a weight belt against the buoyant suit. He hand and knee-walked at an angle away from the shore, struggling to reach deeper water. As the waves washed over his head, he wormed the mask into a tighter fit. In the shallow water, the wind kicked up waves fast, and it was already choppier than before.

Lights swept behind him, as well as the gunfire from pistols and submachine guns. Dugan unconsciously noted the staccato rhythm of AK-47s occasionally sounding flat over the sound of the rain and surf. Had it been a still night, the fleeing agent might not have had a chance. But the rain and the wind-whipped surf hid his retreat long enough for him to get away from the shore. As he breast-stroked and pushed away, fighting the tide that had been so helpful before, he saw that the lights were beginning to congregate at the boathouse.

He could imagine the confusion among men who minutes before had been comfortable, maybe drinking a little, not thinking of trouble. Now they had their sentry yelling about somebody blundering around in the dark.

Well, Dugan thought, *by rights, his pals should be staring at Jose's bloody corpse at this minute. But it wasn't the time, and I'll probably see Jose later anyway.*

While Dugan worked his way out against the tide and the gathering waves, the men from the house finally got to the boathouse, and lights through the windows. The sound of powerful marine engines starting rumbled across the night. Seconds later, a big boat nosed out of the boathouse with a throaty roar, paused, and then surged out into open water.

As Dugan watched warily, his mask just above the surface, the big boat disappeared out into deeper water, then reappeared in a long curve toward the shore, rolling and tossing in the waves, lights flashing from the cockpit. Dugan followed the boat's progress by the roar of the big engines and the white bow wave the boat threw up as it fought the storm, barely under control. Abruptly it slowed, and the boat began a slower search, still plunging and yawing in the increasing waves, but well to the east of where Dugan was. By then, he was comfortably rocking in the waves a quarter mile away and beginning the long swim back to where he'd hidden his car.

Well, we know for certain where they are, he thought, *but now the other side knows somebody else is around, too.*

He took his time in the water. The waves were throwing him around, and the heavy rain made keeping a course hard. Without fins, his progress was slow. But now he was going parallel to the shore, pushed by the incoming tide, and the buoyant wetsuit kept him on the surface, or close enough to it that he didn't have to spend a lot of energy staying afloat.

After about an hour of slow breast stroking, he found the remains of the old pier, and minutes later, the stunted tree with the unobtrusive scrap of white tape on the side facing the water. Just a few yards offshore, he walked easily along the muddy bottom, his body inclined and washed over by the waves and invisible from either land or water. He passed the telltale tape and waded ashore further down the bank, then took a knee to listen.

He heard nothing but the increasing sounds of the storm, so he worked his way back through the woods until he saw the car, wet and shiny in the darkness under a growth of pines and scrub. For half an hour, he stood overwatch, shivering in the woods until he was convinced the car hadn't been compromised. Then he crept cautiously to the rear of the car, found the key under the frame where he'd left it, and as the rain began to turn icy, he stripped off the wetsuit and deactivated the tiny transponder in its molded-in housing on the hood.

Then, almost nude, shivering and exhausted, Dugan climbed into the front seat with just enough energy left to retrieve his cell phone from its hiding place and send a burst to Sal. *I'm here and I'm okay,* the signal said. Then he wrapped himself in the wool blanket he'd laid out beforehand and went to sleep while the tall, dark pines tossed above him, and the rain turned to sleet. *Some pretty bad people are looking for me,* he thought before sleep took him. *We'll meet eventually. No need to rush in exhausted.*

~

Sal and the general followed the events through the feed from the drone. They watched Dugan's chip disappear into the house, reappear, and then the chase, with the heat-blobs of the bad guys milling around in the dark. Sal was unperturbed, and the general took his cue from Sal's poker face.

"He got flushed," Sal explained to the general.

They observed silently as Dugan took to the water and made his slow way back to the car. While the operations center hummed around him and reports came to the general, Sal watched as the little white dot representing Dugan did his surveillance, and when the transponder was turned off and the cell phone burst came in with its coded geolocation, he finally stirred.

"I need a cup of coffee," Sal said. "We'll get a call when he's ready." And he walked away.

Chapter 12

Wednesday 0400

Dugan woke up but kept his eyes closed for ten seconds, gathering strength while the storm blew harder. Then he stirred, picked up the phone, and called Sal. Sal picked it up on the first ring, as Dugan knew he would.

"What's the deal?" he asked.

"They're here," Dugan answered. "Some, anyway." He briefly described the layout and what he could tell of the inhabitants. Sal grunted when Dugan told him about the east Europeans. That might mean something.

"Nice," he said when Dugan finished. Both men knew the conversation was being recorded, and Sal would pass it around later. "We saw the chase. What happened?"

Dugan told him. Sal digested the news in silence. Sal had been doing stuff like this for a long time, and he waited for Dugan's opinion.

"Getting seen is serious, though not a showstopper," Dugan said. "When daylight comes, they might or might not find the fins and snorkel, but this crowd doesn't strike me as people that will wade around in the water looking for clues in this weather." He paused. Despite the lengthy conversation, the information had to be passed. "The NVGs would be the most serious proof that they've got a real player on their hands, and they're deep underwater and unlikely to be found unless somebody steps on them."

"Any contact?" Sal asked.

Dugan knew Sal was really asking if he had to kill anyone.

"No." More silence.

"Pull you in?" Sal asked. With all the ungodly pressure on the little man, he still supported his agent in the field.

Like he always does, Dugan thought. He and Sal went back a long way.

"No," Dugan said. "We don't. They don't know much, and they want to believe everything's still okay. Maybe they'll think it was a local. They've worked too long, and the stakes are too high. They've got a timeline pushing them and the people they're dealing with don't forgive mistakes. They'll tighten up, but they won't bolt."

Sal was silent. Dugan went on. "What they are most likely to do is ramp up security, make it tougher. Tougher on the people they're holding. But the timeline is goosing them in the back; they're on a glide path and they can't change it." Dugan could almost see Sal's deadpan face.

"I need to get closer," Dugan said, "Get inside the town, like we planned." The timer beeped, and he said, "Stand by," and snapped the phone shut. Whoever this was, he had to assume they had technology and too much time on the air could be unhealthy.

The shivering agent unwrapped himself from the scratchy blanket, opened the car door and stepped, barefooted, into the wet pine needles. The sleet had slowed down, but the wind was up and the pines and drip from the trees hit the back of his neck as he fished around in the trunk for his clothes bag. *That timeline cuts both ways,* he thought while he shivered. *They can't stop, and neither can we.*

~

Sal turned to the general and the small operations group that gathered around. He replayed the recording of the conversation and then turned the machine off. There was a silence.

"What have we got on the ships?" he asked.

An airman looked at her smart tablet. "One has announced an intent to anchor off the Norfolk channel on the other side of the Bay Bridge as scheduled," she said. "It altered course to do that. That pretty well takes it out of the running for Baltimore or Washington.

"We still have two potentials. Both headed for the Baltimore channel, both medium-sized freighters, both inspected and passed through the coastal security zone. One will reach our target area tomorrow night at about twenty-two hundred hours, the other about an hour later."

The general looked at Sal. "You know we're cutting it close."

Sal felt a surge of impatience. *No kidding? How the hell do these guys ever win wars,* he thought, immediately regretting it. The general had crash-landed a special operations helo in Afghanistan to rescue a recon team.

Sal turned to his executive assistant standing next to him and said simply, "Get Harvey on the phone for me."

The group stood silently while Sal walked a few feet away to talk to the national security advisor.

56

Chapter 13

Wednesday 0500

Ten minutes later, Dugan had wiped the black cream off his face and dressed in jeans, a wool shirt, work boots, and a windbreaker. In fifteen minutes, the wet suit and mask were in a rubber divers' bag buried in a pile of leaves, and the little knife was in its sheath on his leg. He climbed into the car, got the anonymous Ford turned around, and with the lights off, bounced it down the old logging track to the paved two-lane county road. The road was deserted. He pulled onto the hardtop, switched the lights on, gunned the engine, and turned the heat up.

After all night in the water, Dugan needed something to eat, and he needed a place to finish the conversation with Sal. Ten minutes' drive down the narrow two-lane brought him to an all-night breakfast place at the intersection with the state highway near the outskirts of Stafford, the county seat. It was the only place on the highway with signs of life. There were a few pickup trucks parked outside in the dark, icy rain, and people were sitting at tables.

Dugan pulled up in the gravel parking lot and walked into the lights and warmth. He settled into a booth in the back corner facing the door, just another big man with seamed face and rough work clothes, like the other working men who'd come to the country diner before dawn. He waited until the waitress had taken his order and filled his coffee cup, then flipped open the little black phone. Just another working stiff, up too early, calling the boss. Sal picked it up.

"Yeah," he said.

"I'm going to go in," Dugan said. "I don't see much choice now."

There was a silence on Sal's end. Dugan knew he would have made a decision by now, so the hesitation was bad news.

"Okay," Sal said finally. "The big guys know the deal, and they're giving us lots of leash. But we have movement in the other places. I think it's soon now. The backup team is standing by. But the weather sucks."

Sal was used to juggling operations and dealing with nervous bosses, but he and Dugan both had a healthy respect for real things they couldn't change, like weather.

Dugan glanced out the window. *We're going to have to deal with the reality of a mini-hurricane,* he thought. *This is going to be a full-blown nor'easter, and it's going to make everybody nervous as hell.*

"The weather can work for us, too. These thugs don't look like the kind of people who function very well when it's rough outside." Dugan thought of the old man's eyes in the house. *I'm going to get those bastards.*

"It might raise hell with our comms. Not a lot of backup where you're going."

Dugan refocused. "Got it. But no real choice. Just play it by ear."

"You try telling Winstead we're 'playing it by ear.'"

Dugan grinned. "No sympathy here, Sal. You took the job."

As they talked, Dugan watched a dark SUV drive by the diner for the third time. First time had been just after he had settled into the booth. Second time, slower, when the coffee came, and he had

58

dialed Sal. The third time, the dark SUV drove very slowly past the diner, then u-turned into the parking lot next to Dugan's motor-pool Ford. Two men got out, glanced around the parking lot, and began to walk toward the front door. They didn't look local. The short one in a gray hoodie was clearly Hispanic with short dark hair and medium build. The other was a tall, pale, blond, bodybuilding type in a black windbreaker. They had *goon* written on their faces.

Here we go, Dugan thought, and he took a sip of his coffee.

"Sal," Dugan said, "I've got company. Two bozos headed this way." He gave a quick description as the two mounted the concrete steps to the diner. "I'm in," he said, closing the phone. Then he got interested in the coffee.

The waitress brought over a platter of eggs and hash. "Plate's hot," she said. "Y'all want anything else?" A soft, southern country voice.

Dugan's mind automatically took in all the details. Young for the night shift, about eighteen maybe, blonde and petite, and a little out of place. The ones with a husband and kids usually work nights so they can be home days. *Maybe she's filling in for somebody, or maybe she's married too,* Dugan thought. *No wedding ring, but you can't always tell these days.*

She caught him looking at her ring finger and smiled uncertainly, then moved back toward the front of the diner as the door opened, letting the cold in for a second or two.

The two thugs came in, and the blond guy looked over at Dugan. As their eyes met, he smiled a not-nice smile.

First mistake: telegraphing your punch, Dugan thought. *I wonder what number two will be. Sloppy tradecraft seems to be the standard tonight.*

The two dropped into a booth down the aisle between Dugan and the door. The waitress came back, topped Dugan off, and went away, toward another guy who came in, shaking off water. The coffee, hot and strong, held a trace of the bitter end of a pot that brewed all night. The blond thug drank coffee too. The dark-haired man had a soft drink.

Nobody talked much, and after a time, the waitress found an interesting guy by the cash register. It had been a long night, a cold, wet morning, and it looked to be a long day, so Dugan scraped his plate clean. Outside, the darkness hinted at the first trace of a gray dawn.

Dugan regretfully took the last pull on the third cup. Black, strong coffee was a habit, like the morning shave, left over from the Army. He picked up his check, walking past the two hoods to the cash register. Behind him, they stood up too, as he thought they would, and he sensed them move behind him.

Dugan pulled out his wallet, putting a twenty on the counter. "Keep it," he said to the waitress. "Covers my ugly friends here, too." He gave her a wink. The waitress looked from him to the thugs behind him, sensing the tension. But she took the twenty, and Dugan walked out into the rain. They were close behind him.

They won't pull any triggers in the parking lot, Dugan thought. *Too public, and they don't want to be noticed. My act with the twenty made sure that at least the waitress got a good look at us.*

Halfway to the car, the blond closed up behind Dugan. "Asshole. You go to our car. Quiet. No trouble," he said with an eastern European accent. The dark-haired man said nothing, just shoved a little so Dugan could feel the gun, and the agent relaxed a little.

Amateur mistake. It would have been harder, Dugan knew, if they kept a little distance, out of arm's reach, but close in, it would be easier. The trio got to the SUV. Dugan opened the rear door, climbing quickly into the back seat before the European could give him instructions. The Hispanic looked at the European, shrugged, and followed Dugan into the back seat, showing his gun for the first time. The European got in the front to drive.

I'm behind the driver, Dugan thought, *and they don't seem to have a problem with that. Or that this punk is sitting in easy arm's reach.*

The Hispanic sensed Dugan's threat and lifted his pistol until it pointed at Dugan's head. Dugan nodded minutely to indicate cooperation, and the pistol dropped to his midsection. The door slammed, and the interior light went off. *Easier and easier.*

The driver gunned the engine, and they swayed and jerked getting onto the highway. They drove about a quarter mile down the rain-swept road, then turned quickly onto what felt like a rutted farm track. Nobody talked. As the car lurched around in the dark, Dugan palmed the little long-bladed knife out of his ankle sheath on the left-hand side, away from the man beside him.

On the next pothole, Dugan twisted and fell against the Hispanic, pushing the gun away with his right hand. His left came across his body and drove the skinny little blade under the man's chin and into his brain. The pistol exploded in the dark with a blinding flash of light and heat, and the windshield shattered. The man stiffened, made a bubbling sound from his lips, and gave a little convulsive jerk of his legs.

Dugan, ears ringing from the blast, saw the blond grabbing for the gun he had probably put on the seat beside him. He didn't find it before Dugan's right hand had grabbed his jaw and jerked his head around. The little knife went in behind the driver's ear, up into the brain just like his partner. The car slammed into a ditch, the airbags went off with a bang, and as quickly, deflated.

Dugan bailed out of the car into the drizzle, dazed, half-deaf from the shot, and half-blinded by the muzzle flash. The cold hit him like a blow. He felt the rain beating on his face as he shook his head and spun quickly around to the car, but the two men were dead, or nearly so. The European made some last twitches, but as Dugan watched, the big man groaned and died.

In the dim light, Dugan could see blood everywhere. He leaned on the car, closing his eyes for several heartbeats. *Close,* he thought. *Too damn close.* Then he really looked at the SUV. The car was nose-down in a drainage ditch, the windshield in fragments, and the vehicle's bumper pushed against a gnarled pine. The motor still ran, trying to push the tree over.

Dugan reached across the dead body in the driver's seat and cut off the engine. The scene suddenly got quiet, save for the sound of the sleety rain bouncing off Dugan's windbreaker. He looked around, seeing nothing but the rutted track and a line of dark pines tossing and bending in the wind.

Dugan guessed this lane used to lead to a plantation house or a local farmhouse, set well back and leading to a dirt road to town. Now with the old house gone and the pine trees lining the lane, it was a good place to pull off and drink underage beer or neck a little. This morning though, it was a good place for murder.

Dugan let the car door swing shut on its own. The rain mixed with sleet, but it had slacked a little. He could see gray shapes around him in the early dawn. The paved road was not far away, and it was still deserted, but from it a passing motorist could easily see the SUV jammed at an angle into the ditch.

What we don't need is some guy in a four-wheel pickup with a winch on the bumper to stop and offer me a hand getting out, Dugan thought. He opened the door again, put his hands under driver's shoulders, and pulled him from behind the wheel, grunting with the dead weight.

Once the corpse's feet had cleared the doorframe, Dugan dropped him in the mud. As the body fell, a black clamshell cell phone slid out of a shirt pocket, landing in a clump of wet grass. Dugan bent down and popped it open. It was the cheap, convenience store model used by drug dealers and philandering lovers to conceal calls. He snapped it shut and stuck it in his pocket.

Crossing to the other side, Dugan did the same with the smaller guy. The angle of the stuck car made it easier, and when he opened the back door, the man pitched out on his own. Dugan dragged him by the ankles through the mud to the ditch a little way down from the car. Then he did the same with the European, dragging him around the back of the car and dumping him next to his partner.

Dugan didn't expect to find much in their pockets, but he did the search anyway. The blond had a few twenties, which Dugan put back in the dead man's pocket. Sal's people would be sent in to go over the car and these bodies for clues as to who sent them. Sometimes money talked in unexpected ways.

The driver's 9mm had rattled down into the floorboards, and Dugan left it there. The dark-haired man still gripped his pistol in his right hand, his muscles frozen in a last spasm. Dugan left it alone and straightened up. He was a little surprised that, as sloppy as their tradecraft was, they at least had known not to carry anything identifiable. *So there are some rules,* he thought. *Somebody in charge. That's something to remember.*

He went back to the SUV, leaving the two corpses piled in a muddy heap in the ditch with the rain beating down on their upturned faces and wide eyes. Blood was splattered around the inside of the car, so Dugan used his knife to cut away the airbags, using the silver fabric to cover the driver's seat well enough to keep him out of the gore. When he finished, he had blood on his hands and his shirt. He wiped his hands in the wet grass and made a mental note to change shirts when he got to his car.

Getting behind the wheel, he started the engine and engaged the four-wheel drive. After some rocking back and forth, he got the SUV out of the ditch. He backed it down the lane of trees to the highway, stopped, flipped open his little phone and punched in Sal's access code. Dugan hit the send button and Sal answered.

"I'm going to talk fast," Dugan said. The call was recorded, anyway. "Two bodies in a ditch. I'll hit the GPS."

Sal said nothing, though he may have grunted.

"They must have some kind of direction-finder," Dugan continued. "I'm going to dump their SUV and their cell phone at a diner down the road. It's in no shape to be found by the locals." Dugan knew Sal had specialists who could exploit the information stored in the cell phone's brain, and he would get agents to the diner to take possession of the SUV before the local police were attracted by the shattered windshield and the blood on the seats, not to mention the 9mm on the floor.

Sal also knew better than to waste words. "We have the ships. They're about fourteen hours out." Things were speeding up.

"I'm going to the town," Dugan said. "Fourteen hours gives us a little time. What else?"

"Backup?" Sal asked.

"Just what we planned," Dugan said. "We still don't know what they've got in the town, or what they've got at the B and B. The muscle today was amateur stuff. Maybe that's important."

"Okay," Sal said and clicked off.

Dugan punched in a combination of numbers that sent a global positioning burst so Sal could send a team to collect the two bodies. Later in the morning, the two dead men would be on the way to an autopsy, and then to a discrete funeral home for cremation. Their ashes would be dumped down a toilet.

With the heater full on and the rain blowing through the jagged holes where the windshield had been, Dugan drove the dark SUV back to the parking lot, stopping on the other side of the Ford. Wet and cold in the gray morning, he took a minute in the SUV to look at the blond European's pistol, a standard, black, Beretta M9, fourteen shots in the clip.

Noting the serial number on the receiver, Dugan knew Sal's guys could probably trace it down. *Their tradecraft looks worse and worse. This is a pickup team, and they obviously weren't expecting competition. But there's enough supervision on the ground to make them empty their pockets,* he thought.

He tossed the pistol and the cell phone behind the seat and left the keys in the SUV's ignition. Then he walked across the parking lot in the rain, fishing his own keys out of his pocket, and drove the Ford away—cold, wet, and thirsty for another cup of coffee. The diner was out of the question, but he remembered a franchise hamburger place a few miles down the road from the diner. When he got there, it was just opening for the day. He pulled around to the drive thru. When he got to the window, he handed the kid inside another twenty and his old dented thermos to fill with coffee.

The wind picked up. The rain and sleet came down slantwise. Even in the car, it felt colder.

Chapter 14

Wednesday 0800

Dugan took the flat, two-lane road winding through the farm country back toward Brewer and the bay. The pavement was shiny black and deserted in the early morning. The fields and scrub forest on either side were brown and forlorn looking as the rain and wind whipped across them. The naked trees looked dark with the wet, but the occasional stands of pine kept some color.

Now and then an old, two-story, white, frame house would sit back from the road in a grove of hardwoods, or a doublewide up on a cinderblock foundation would sit alone in a field, a pickup truck next to it on a gravel driveway. There was nearly always a boat on a trailer in the yard or behind the house.

This part of Virginia had thus far escaped the rush for waterfront development that lined the river to the north. *Scratching a living off farming and working the bay is still a way of life around here,* Dugan mused as the brown fields rolled by. *The waitress in the diner probably lived somewhere near in a place like this. Life out here will have a different rhythm, or at least it used to. But these places die hard.*

While the car heater dried him out and warmed him, Dugan started concentrating on the opposition and what they were thinking. He wasn't too worried that missing two foot-soldiers would spook this crowd. He guessed they sent out the hired help—low-level thugs, tough enough for the job of pushing civilians around, but either too dumb or too careless, to take on the first team. *Which would be me,* he thought. Their bosses would take some time to realize they weren't coming back, and even then, they would be uncertain about the cause. They would probably take hours to come to any kind of conclusion, and by then events would be moving fast. Or so Dugan hoped.

Sal and Dugan figured the top people running this end of the operation were hard-core Zetas, but Dugan now believed most of the troops were pickups up from east coast gangs that owed the bosses a favor or two. That would account for the ethnic mix of the Ukrainian or Chechens, Mexicans and Salvadorans, as well as sloppy operations.

The boss can only supervise so much, Dugan thought. *He can enforce things like empty pockets, but not what his pickup team does when they're on their own. And there was confusion at the Walker House last night. Poor control. These are city punks, used to roughing up storeowners or pimps, but not accustomed to real fieldwork.*

But Dugan also knew tracking him to the diner indicated a little more sophistication. He took a pull of coffee from his thermos cup. *Somebody sent them out. Probably the boss, who came to find out what all the noise was about. He's probably staying at the bed and breakfast, separate from his troops. He'd been good enough to pick up on a secured cell transmission and act on it fast. The cheap guns meant hired muscle, but the intercept technology and the quick reaction means that somebody's a pro, and that the boss and his electronics are probably in the bed and breakfast.*

Dugan looked for a place to pull off. A few miles from Brewer, he found an abandoned service station on the right side of the road with a potholed driveway that went around back. The place had obviously been closed for years, with broken windows and weeds sprouting from cracks in the concrete.

He parked behind the building, where the car was hidden from anyone passing by. Climbing out, he popped the trunk and pulled out a worn duffel. Stripping again in the icy rain, he threw the bloody shirt and tee shirt he'd been wearing into the weeds behind the station and got back in the car bare-chested. While the engine idled, he dug through the bag and pulled out a dry tee and a heavy wool shirt. He slipped the tee over his head, struggled into the shirt, set his watch alarm, and dropped the seat. The sound of the rain beating on the windshield put him to sleep immediately.

Thirty minutes later, Dugan's watch woke him, and he shook off the cobwebs. The beat of the rain continued, and the inside of his mouth was dry as he fumbled for his thermos and more coffee. Five minutes later, he lurched and bumped the car around the old service station and back to the road.

The clouds were even lower, and rain lashed across the blacktop. He felt the car shudder as the wind gusts hit it. The road was mostly deserted in the thin gray light.

Dugan slowed the car in the rain and began watching for the farm road on the left. If the overheads were right, Brewer was less than a mile ahead, just beyond the ridge and the next row of trees. The farm road appeared, and Dugan swung the car off the highway.

A hundred years ago, when the Chesapeake Bay held enough crabs and oysters to support a thousand watermen in their flat-bottomed boats, small towns that made their fortune from the bay's bounty dotted the shore. Local warehouses bought the watermen's catch, peeled the crabs, shucked the oysters, and then shipped them to markets in Baltimore and Washington. But when the catches dropped off, the towns shriveled up.

The old warehouses and shucking sheds still stood here and there, slowly decaying, with their rickety docks and old boats rotting in the marshes. Brewer, tucked away on the base of a neck of land, was a town like that, a sad little collection of weathered buildings at the end of the road, past the sign that said state maintenance stopped here and where the pavement ended at the waterfront and the deserted old shucking house.

According to the overheads Dugan studied and the information Sal's people collected, the only business in town was a filling station attached to a restaurant that probably sold bait and fishing gear on the side. There wasn't much to say for the town, except about a hundred people still lived there who wrung a living from the bay and farming. It was on a neck of land jutting out where the Potomac River joined the Chesapeake, putting it on the water routes to both Baltimore and Washington.

It was probably the most isolated place in this part of the state—no cable, no wireless, and weak cellphone coverage. Perfect for kidnapping and possibly murder—perfect, in fact, for the people Sal and Dugan hunted.

Dugan eased the Ford along the squishy track through standing water and mud, hoping that he could get the car out again when the time came. Just for a moment, he regretted the four-wheel he'd abandoned in the parking lot

When the highway was out of sight, he found the dirt track that had showed faintly on the satellite photos, and he turned right into a stand of pine trees where the needles and sandy soil gave the car better traction than the mud. The scrub oaks concealed the car from the farm road and the highway. He killed the engine and sat for a minute, watching the steady rain hit the windshield, a little less steadily now that the car was among trees.

He was tired. No matter what shape he was in, a man on the north side of thirty-five has a tough time with midnight swims and not much sleep. Without getting out of the car, he looked around. The woods were deserted in all directions. He checked again to be sure his knife was secure in its ankle sheath, pulled out his cell phone, and dialed up the GPS feature.

From somewhere in his memory, Dugan typed in the coordinates he needed and watched the little purple line swing around off to his right. Two miles and a few decimals. Then he slid the seat back, raised the floor mat, and pushed at just the right spot. The lid lifted on the flat compartment, and Dugan took out the .45 and a spare magazine.

Sal gave his field agents wide discretion in what kind of armament to use and when to carry it. As a rule, Dugan preferred not to go armed, since having a gun could be awkward if a cop wanted to do a stop and search. There were plenty of times when a gun just didn't feel right for his role of the moment. Because he was a big man, he had always counted on muscle and reflexes to get himself out of tight corners. So far it had worked. He thought briefly of his encounter with the two men that morning. A gun wouldn't have helped him there.

But what he was about to do was different, and his experience told him it was time for his old M1911, the granddaddy of automatic pistols, invented by Mr. Colt over a century ago to fight Philippine tribesmen. He hefted the heavy pistol, liking its sturdy feel and looks.

He knew all the arguments against using this particular weapon. The heavy magazine only held seven rounds, and it had to be cocked for the first shot. There were more modern pistols, but when that big 230-grain bullet went loping out there, the fight was usually over. He had seen people hit with a 9mm who just kept coming. Didn't happen with a .45. He checked the clip, worked the slide to crank a round into the chamber, eased down the hammer, and stuck the extra magazine in his left-hand hip pocket.

He took his wallet out of his right-hand pocket and stuck it in the glove compartment. Nothing was in it anyway but a fake driver's license, some credit cards in another man's name, and some cash, but he was a professional. He opened the door and stepped out of the car into the windy cold. Under the trees, the rain wasn't as steady, but the water dripped through the pine needles.

Dugan crammed the pistol—butt out—in his right-hand hip pocket. He slipped the phone in a front pocket, stripped off the light windbreaker he'd been wearing, and pulled a dark wool jacket, black knit cap, and fingerless black wool gloves out of the duffel bag.

Wool would be quiet in the woods, had the great advantage of being warm when wet, and would help him fight the chill that had already begun to seep into his body. The car's heater had done its best, but his jeans were still damp from earlier in the morning, and they turned cold almost immediately.

At least I've got good boots and dry feet, he thought, *or at least they'll start out that way.* He took out the black stocking cap and pushed the small button that activated the miniature transmitter woven into the top of the cap. The device was so small and lightweight that a casual search would miss it, but Sal's overhead drones would be able to detect the infinitesimal signal. He pulled on the cap and gloves, flexing his fingers as he did so.

Dugan carried nothing that could be traced. The phone did not retain a record of calls, and its GPS had only one location in its memory. The phone's electronics would fuse if the wrong entry code was used. A talented gunsmith who worked for Sal had erased the pistol's serial number years ago. Dugan had nothing in his pockets—no stray receipts, no notecards, not even pocket change. Every agent knew the story of the British counterintelligence ring back during the Irish Troubles, massacred by the IRA because they had been careless about tradecraft and left pocket paper around— receipts, theater stubs, impressions on hotel stationary—for the opposition to collect.

After years in the business, Dugan instinctively left no trail. He carried no paper, paid with cash, and sanitized his hotel rooms when he left. The habit was so ingrained that he slipped through life leaving as little trace as possible. He was occasionally lonely but accepted a solitary life as the price of his profession.

This job was no different, except the stakes were so high. He was operating on home turf for the first time in his life. He knew that his agency was barred by law from operating in the U.S., but Sal took care of that formality with a quick oath, administered by a grim-faced judge, and an FBI badge that Dugan had left in Sal's care.

So he had legal cover, though that wouldn't be much good if the other side got their hands on him. If they caught him today, all they would gather is that he wasn't a tourist; the little knife, the .45, and the absence of any identification would tell them that, but they wouldn't know anything else. *The idea,* Dugan thought, *is not to get caught.*

He checked the little phone's GPS again, looking through the pines and scrubby oaks ahead. He worked a telltale pin oak leaf into the seam between the trunk and the body of the car. Then he did the same thing with the doors and the hood in front, stopped, and took a deep breath. He was ready.

With a final glance around, Dugan stepped off into the woods in the direction indicated by the phone's GPS. The woods here were the usual southern tangle of scrub oak and low pines, growing where a field had probably been twenty or thirty years before. The sandy ground was covered with the year's fall of leaves and patches of weeds and vines. Dugan worked left and right, leaving as few tracks as possible.

He moved slowly, as hunters do in the woods, pausing every hundred feet or so to drop to one knee and listen, mouth slightly open, head moving from side to side to catch the slightest sound. Even with the wind and rain, sound would carry, and it would even carry farther on a wet day. It was slow going, and shortly the chill began to penetrate the jacket, but he ignored the discomfort. He couldn't afford to rush. Not yet.

The ground began to slope gradually up, and the trees changed to tall pines and big oaks. A faint trail wandered through the woods and headed roughly in the same direction he was headed. Dugan drew back into the brush, knelt, and considered. Game trails were fairly frequent in these woods. From what he remembered of growing up in the rural south, he imagined the local deer would have a pretty hard time with some of the residents of Brewer, but since it was headed in the same direction he was going, he decided this trail was worth following.

He moved cautiously parallel to it, still on slowly rising ground, well back in the trees, keeping behind what cover he could. He followed the stop-and-listen protocol he'd been taught until it was instinctive. Movement was slow, but he wasn't in enough of a hurry to take dumb chances.

After thirty minutes, he fell further back in the trees, went to one knee out of sight of the trail, and checked the distance on the GPS. About a mile to go. The ground rose more steeply now. The oaks thinned out to be replaced by tall pines whose needles made a carpet on the ground and further deadened sound and hid his tracks. The ground cover thinned out, too. He moved back toward the trail and was about to resume his movement uphill when the sound of voices to his right sent a shock through his system.

Dugan froze, then as the voices drew nearer, he very slowly sank to the ground, making no hurried movements, drawing the .45 slowly while easing behind a patch of scrub growing to his left. The trail was about twenty or thirty feet away with a few scrubby bushes and a big pine in front of him. He sank down behind the scrub. Once his chest was on the ground, he eased one of his gloved hands in front of his shiny white face and watched through his fingers, while the second gripped the pistol low behind the bushes.

The sound of the voices had stopped, but he could hear two or three walkers approaching his hiding position. They were walking on the trail, and—Dugan hoped—unaware that he was spread flat in the leaves a few yards away. Their voices were conversational, not alarmed, and he heard a snorting laugh in response to a joke.

As always when things got tense, Dugan's senses seemed to expand and fill the space around him. He heard the leaves dripping and the sound of their footsteps, and he could feel the shape of his pistol's grip in his right hand. He cocked the hammer back, flattened his body against the ground, and tried to look small. In less than a minute, the men appeared on the trail to his right, walking across his vision, following the uphill trail.

There were three of them, walking in a loose group, and fortunately not paying much attention to the woods around them. One wore a parka with his hood up against the rain, and the other two wore baseball hats. They looked uncomfortable and unhappy to be outside in this god-awful weather, hands jammed in pockets, shoulders hunched against the cold.

Good for me, Dugan thought.

The one who appeared to be the leader featured the blond hair and flat, Slavic features similar to the man Dugan had left in the ditch a few hours earlier. The other two were darker in complexion and probably Latinos. The blond seemed to have a sidearm in a leather holster beneath his short jacket. The other two were armed with what appeared to be Heckler and Koch MP5Ks, short, nasty-looking 9mm submachine guns favored by commandos and wannabes the world 'round. They were room-cleaners with very high rates of fire. If it came to a shootout, Dugan knew he would have very little chance with a mere pistol.

So much for the .45, he thought. He watched them walk by with their collars turned up, eyes on the trail, and body language that said they'd be happy to get the patrol over with and get out of the wet.

More of the temporary help, Dugan thought. *Far from their comfortable slum rooms and pool halls in the city.*

They ambled by with their slung weapons pointed at the ground, and as they got closer, Dugan saw that the one with the hoodie wore earbuds in with wires running into the pocket of his brown jacket. As they passed out of sight range, he caught a guttural word in what might have been English. One of them, probably the one without the earbuds, gave another short laugh.

Dugan lay prone for five full minutes, giving them plenty of time to pass and for his pounding heart to slow. *Too close.* He was taking himself to task. He knew it was only by chance that they'd spoken in enough time for him to get behind cover. He was nearly caught at the old mansion the previous night, and then the opposition picked him up electronically earlier in the morning. And now he'd almost been caught by three greenhorns who couldn't find their way out of the woods with a signpost.

I'm close to screwing this up by the numbers, he thought. *Take it easy, pal. Lots of time to get killed later. It's early in the game, yet.*

Chapter 15

Dugan assumed the disappearance of the two thugs from that morning hadn't raised an alarm, or these guys wouldn't have been sleepwalking through the woods. If the three on foot patrol had any idea their two buddies were headed for a metal slab somewhere in Maryland, they'd have been alert, to say the least.

He stood and kept the .45 in his right hand. He eased the hammer down and began moving, now using the slow, sliding movement of the old recon teams in close contact: mouth open to help his ears, eyes scanning up and down, left and right, the pistol following his eyes, slowly moving through the thin underbrush, brain picking out hiding positions every thirty feet or so, and automatically coming to a listening stop every twenty paces. As he moved and watched, he tried to put himself in his adversary's mind.

By now, the boss might a little concerned about his detail's failure to report in. But there could have been delays in getting rid of my body and stopping for a celebratory cup of coffee after a morning's work well done. They probably would be minimizing cell phone calls. Even after the two became obviously overdue, say an hour or two from now, there'd be uneasiness, but no certainty that the feds—that would be me, among others—were coming down on their little operation. I still have time before things speed up. Remember, he's on a timeline that he can't stop.

Dugan had no illusions about the top people in this operation. They might have hired low-level talent for their muscle, but the bosses and their inner circles would be pros. They could add things up, but Dugan expected, as long as they weren't sure what was going on, they would hold to their schedule.

A lot depends on that guess, he thought, *because I surely threw some sand in their gears this morning.*

The rain still came down, but under the forest canopy, Dugan was only damp. Correction, cold and damp. As he moved and thought, his listening, scanning, and pace counting went on automatic. That part of his mind picked out and inspected trees, shrubs, and bushes on his route that his conscious brain was only half-aware of, just as the fingers of a musician playing a familiar score seem to move on their own.

Dugan had learned to stalk in the deep woods of the south. His later instructors had decided he was a natural, and the jobs he and Sal had done over the years had polished his skills. Stalking had become second nature, so as he counted steps and slid around branches and downed limbs, part of his mind weighed his opponent's defenses.

If these guys are so technically savvy that they're running their own cellphone interception net out in the boondocks, then they'll have something else closer in that's more dependable than the hired help tromping along the trails.

The slope of the ground increased as Dugan moved, still paralleling the trail, and he sensed he would soon come to the top of the ridge that, according to the satellite pictures, should overlook the bed and breakfast where he and Sal guessed at least some of the gang were staying. *They'll be looking for high ground for their communications,* he thought. *Plus, it's a more comfortable place for the brass. But they'll have more security out than just a bunch of thugs strolling through the woods.* Then he saw the camera.

The giveaway was a glint in a pine tree where no glint should be, and a black bump against brown bark about fifteen feet up. Dugan stopped still, and after a moment, very slowly sank to the ground while he focused on what looked like a small video camera looking back down the trail. Did it see him? Even though it appeared to be focused on the trail, surveillance cameras normally come with a wide field of view, and he couldn't estimate what this one saw. He was at a good thirty-degree offset, and he couldn't see the lens directly. Dugan decided to chance it.

A slow sweep of his head and eyes didn't find any others or a convenient place to put one. The pine tree that held the one visible camera stood mostly apart from the other scrubby foliage. Normally, he knew, these things would be employed in overlapping bands, but perhaps the opposition here wasn't using them the way the manufacturer's handbook suggested.

He heard no sounds except the wind in the treetops and the drip of water onto the leaves. He waited for what felt like an hour, which logically was probably only ten minutes, for any sign or sound of alarm. Nothing.

At the end of his waiting time, he slowly, very slowly, eased away from the trail and away from the direction of the camera's lens. Half crouching, half creeping, he moved ten yards around the camera. With his left hand extended at ground level, his fingers brushed a wire stretched taut and horizontally about six inches above the ground.

Once again, he froze while the old proverb about *never cut a taut wire and never pull a slack one* ran through his head. He wasn't about to cut this one or pull it either, for that matter. The wire ran from a stake to his left across to the other side of the trail. Rather than going around and finding more traps, he cat-footed closer to the wire. Careful not to touch it again, Dugan eased one leg at a time over. When he was fully over the wire, he looked down on it. In the brush on the left he could just make out a black square device with what might have been a short antenna sticking out the top, and Dugan recognized the ground sensor, designed to send a signal if the tripwire was disturbed.

That makes sense, he thought. *I've seen arrangements with explosive devices, but around here killing a deer or two might bring in unwanted attention.* Kneeling in the brush, he again looked very carefully around. This one was set up to catch wayfarers off the trail.

Dugan knew there were dozens of surveillance and anti-intrusion gadgets out on the open market, from night vision goggles to hidden surveillance cameras and even seismic motion detectors that could detect a footstep half a mile away. From the foot patrols, camera, and tripwires, it was obvious the opposition had every expectation of having their privacy respected. These devices were simple enough for anyone to put in place, so they probably didn't even need to use a technician to have them installed. They only needed a wireless network, and this far out of commercial range, that meant they had to set up their own.

But all plans have holes, Dugan knew. They put patrols in the woods, and they were sloppy. He had a hunch the people he stalked were in a hurry—city boys not comfortable in the woods and not experienced with setting cameras and other electronic sensors in these conditions. They only focused their cameras on trails.

They built a security cordon to last only long enough for the job, and they were in too much of a hurry to be thorough. With their ship barely twelve hours away, they would be focused on getting the job done and prone to making mistakes.

That might be good for me, Dugan thought, *but it might be murder for the hostages.*

The woods thinned out ahead as he approached the top of the ridge in his gorilla crouch. He paused behind a clump of brush to scan ahead and thankfully saw no high trees or security poles mounted on the ridge itself. Easing slowly onto all fours in the wet pine needles, Dugan very carefully worked his way to a place just below the ridgetop, getting lower and lower on hands and knees until finally crawling the last few feet to the top, stopping behind a big pine with some scrubby bushes at the base. Taking a second to catch his breath and listen to the faint sounds of conversation drifting up, he cautiously peered around the tree trunk at the scene below. A car door slammed in the distance and an engine started up.

The tree line ended on the top of the ridge. Below him, the ground sloped away into a long meadow, the spiky grass now brown and wet in the persistent, slanting rain, dropping gently down for a hundred yards before it flattened out onto a broad shelf. A quarter of a mile further, it dropped again to the water's edge.

On the shelf sat an old Victorian-style house, facing to Dugan's right, surrounded by a lawn in its winter brown and a circular driveway with two black SUVs parked by the steps leading to the front porch. Behind it stood an outbuilding of some kind and an old Jeep station wagon. Down the slope from the porch, a pier stretched out a short distance into a creek, with a channel through the brown reeds and brushes in the shallow water to the deeper waters of the bay.

In the far distance, the gray waters of the Chesapeake Bay covered the horizon. Here where the bay met the Potomac, there was enough water for an ocean. Dugan knew Brewer was about a mile away on his right. The house faced toward town. In past years when most of the land was farmed, the town and the old deserted house where he had gone for a swim the previous night would have been visible.

Even allowing for the trees that now hid the town and the cold, gray rain, the view of the bay was spectacular. In better weather, with the sun sparkling on the water and the grass green, it would be a peaceful, idyllic scene, though the ominous-looking SUVs marred the peaceful view, and the plank roughly nailed up along the front corner of the house clashed with the historic décor of the old, well-maintained building. The four-by-four projected above the eaves and supported a long metal rod, like the ones on the old TV antennas, with a white plastic globe on the end. An antenna lead ran into an upstairs window, and two guide wires ran down from the makeshift tower to stakes in the ground, driven unevenly. It was sloppy but good enough for its purpose.

Dugan decided he was looking at a local-area cell phone tower. It probably also included the antenna for the intercept capability the heavies used to track him down earlier that the morning.

The SUVs in front of the house were black, mud-splattered, with knobby tires, just like the one he'd taken earlier. Whoever had been slamming car doors was gone. Figuring four to a car, there were as many as twelve people at the house or driving around.

The rain fell steadily on the exposed house and the grounds around it. The wind gusted in from the water, tossing the grasses and raising whitecaps even in the sheltered little bay down at the water's edge. Dugan settled on his stomach behind a pine and the low bushes at its base, which would break the wind and hide his face. And waited.

His vantage point gave him a sweeping view of the Chesapeake Bay where it meets the Potomac. The distance from his hiding place on the ridge across the bay to the Eastern Shore was about thirty miles. The gray water melded with the gray and overcast sky to make the horizon almost invisible. Even with the blowing rain and low clouds, he could see a distant tug pulling a heavy barge toward Annapolis or Baltimore and the white specks of the sheets of water the storm threw against the tug's bow.

The Chesapeake's deep channels, scoured by natural tides, run north from the bay's mouth in the Atlantic Ocean to Baltimore and beyond. Dugan knew that when seagoing traffic left the central channel to voyage up the great rivers that fed the bay—the James,

York, Rappahannock, and Potomac—the navigation became more challenging.

To Dugan's left was the Potomac, so deep and broad at its mouth that the junction of the river and the bay resembled the ocean sixty miles away. But further to his left, upstream, the Potomac River channel became more and more constricted as it began to twist and turn like a typical southern river as it approached Washington D.C. A century ago, a thriving shipping trade to Alexandria existed. Now only the occasional naval ship sailed for the Washington Navy Yard. Aside from that, not much.

The go-fast was a smart decision, Dugan thought. *It'll be able to navigate the turns and shallows at high speed to the District, and the freighter can stay in the straight channel all the way to Baltimore.*

Dugan was down low under the wind, and after ten minutes he began to get damply comfortable, despite the chill rain. Too comfortable, he realized with a start as he began to doze off. *Damn!* he thought. *I wouldn't have done that a few years ago.*

He made a fist with his thumb jammed under his chin to warn against nodding off. He raised his eyes from the house and looked over the gray Potomac, where streaks of whitecaps appeared and disappeared in the growing waves. In better weather, the horizon would have been dotted with the white hulls of crabbers and oystermen, going about life on the water. But no small boats sailed today. Thirty knots of wind whipped up four and five-foot seas in the broad waters. It was a wild and threatening scene, while above him, the pines moaned and swayed in the wind. Below, the marsh grasses rippled and swayed, a kaleidoscope of constantly changing browns. In summer or on tranquil days, the house commanded a beautiful view of sunrise over the bay. Today it was nature untamed. And the two black SUVs below him in the driveway underscored the threatening note.

Long stalks take a certain kind of concentration, with the patience that comes from much practice. After years of practice, Dugan was able to focus on a target hour after hour while a part of his mind roamed free, like a bored long-distance highway driver who would be instantly alert at a bump on the road. Earlier in his life, in sniper school, he learned to lay patiently for hours and days, unmoving, waiting for that split-second to take a shot. Good shooters learn to wait in many places–jungle trails, city street corners, apartment windows facing a certain way, blacked-out cars parked outside nightclubs.

Policemen knew the hours and hours of boredom on stakeouts, and in some ways, Dugan's business wasn't that different. His life was more solitary, which he accepted, though his body had started to complain a little. He kept his thumb under his chin to stay alert and thought of kitchen tables out of the rain and cups of hot coffee.

Chapter 16

Wednesday 1000

"He's in overwatch," said Sal, squinting at the little white blob on the gray screen. He took a sip of his coffee, remembering the feel of the ground, the smells, and the weather. While he watched, the Air Force three-star talked low-voiced with the staff and moved quietly from one computer screen to another, assessing the progress of the two ships as they approached the mouth of the bay. The general redirected the tracks of the overhead sensors, updating the network of intelligence specialists.

At the last minute, orders had gone out, conveyed personally from the director of Homeland Security to the commandant of the Coast Guard, to ease up on the inspections and let the ships through the coastal defense zone. The Coast Guard boarding team's initial effort to identify the target ship by concealed radiation detectors reported negative findings.

Sal's first attempt to identify the suspect ship failed, but he never had much confidence the boarding parties would be effective anyway. Sal had learned in a hard school not to underestimate the enemy, and he was certain this opponent would have anticipated the boarding parties, which were randomly but routinely conducted on ships approaching the U.S. Sal assumed some method of effective radiation shielding would conceal the bogus cargo.

As the inspection teams finished their work and reported their findings, the Coast Guard cleared the ships' courses through the Baltimore Channel. Each ship approaching the gap in the bridge-tunnel was required to pick up a bay pilot to guide the passage through the bridge-tunnel and up the bay to Baltimore. The requirement to pick up a bay pilot had given Sal his second—and in his mind, the most likely—opportunity to identify the target firsthand.

While his deputy sorted out the ships' progress, Sal watched Dugan on the big screen and reviewed the net he was attempting to cast. Uneasiness gnawed on his mind. The operation was planned too rapidly with too many moving parts. They didn't have any options, and sometimes you just had to go with what you have and play it by ear.

Winstead would shit a brick if he heard that, Sal thought. *He thinks we've got it all figured. But calling plays from scrimmage is really our best bet. Our only bet, now.*

The operations team was still working out some of the plan's final details. There were still ten hours before the ships were actually in the channel—not long, but maybe long enough. Failure must not be contemplated. There were great risks, but he respected the president's willingness to run them and not to simply write off a hundred people.

Sal knew it was always about people, and his were the best. He sipped his coffee and returned to watching Dugan on the screen.

~

Probably a few hours passed. It was hard for Dugan to tell, and he didn't want to move his arm to check his watch. He focused on a trickle of water running down his right calf. The door below slammed open, and three men came out followed by a woman. She stumbled as if shoved, and once she regained her balance, turned her back on the men and on him, looking toward the bay in the distance.

Three more men filed onto the porch. But one man in particular caught Dugan's eye. He was a big man with gray, slicked-back hair, giving abrupt orders to an underling in a language that sounded to Dugan like explosive Spanish, even from this distance. Dugan recognized the leader from Sal's mission brief—Felix Guzmann.

A product of Guatemala by way of the Guatemala City gangs, Mexico City, New Jersey, and Baltimore, Guzmann was said to be a rising star in the Zetas. Everything Dugan saw about him set Guzmann apart from his street soldiers on the porch. Big, running to fat, and gray-haired, he projected an air of superiority over the younger, rougher-cut thugs that Dugan had seen thus far. Guzmann was not in the jeans and bomber jackets of his employees, but rather stylishly dressed in tan slacks of some kind, a dark turtleneck, and a dark brown sport coat, maybe leather.

Guzmann's deputies were unfamiliar to Dugan. They most likely came out of the local gangs. MS-13 was big in northern Virginia. Probably there for the money, they looked brutal. Like Guzmann, they may have all been products of Guatemala, but their route was by way of the slums of San Salvador, Tegucigalpa, and Los Angeles, rather than the higher, swankier road Guzmann had taken. They were short by comparison—squatty to his height; lanky black hair instead of the slicked-back gray.

Dugan thought of the woman being pushed around and felt a sudden reckless urge to go down to the house. *Not now,* he thought. *Not like this.*

After a minute, the big man's assistant began barking at the other four. Dugan was experienced with work details and sensed the boss was handing out orders for the day. The straw boss was adding details, and the work force was taking them.

Dugan recognized one of the three who'd passed him in the woods on their careless patrol. The other two had to be somewhere else, maybe on the next shift.

Or they may be tracking me at this moment. He imagined someone coming up the woods in his unprotected rear. He dismissed the possibility, remembering the discomfort of the three on patrol. It was far more likely, he decided, they would be in the house, resting from their turn at sentry.

While the foot soldiers asked questions and the straw boss settled details with his subordinates, the boss grabbed the arm of the aloof woman, jerked her around, and said something that made everybody laugh. She pulled away, and he pushed her hard into one of the baseball-hat thugs who grabbed her and pushed her to somebody else, just like low-class delinquents in high school.

She shook free and hurried to the corner of the porch. The bullying might have gone further and gotten nastier but a shouted phrase from the boss quieted them down. Dugan spoke passable Spanish, but the distance was a problem. The gist of what he thought he heard was "business first, play later."

Dugan didn't know if the woman spoke Spanish, but he wouldn't have given a dime for her chances of coming out of this alive without his help. These people did not leave witnesses. And he couldn't guarantee that if he got her out alive, she'd be in any shape to be grateful.

The rushed briefing he'd received before beginning this mission taught him that, over two centuries ago, the house had been a plantation manor house with wide fields and its own deep-water pier for loading tobacco. After the Civil War, the plantations were split up, and the house became the home of a local judge and his family. Several changes of ownership later, the house had been modernized and split up into guest bedrooms by the new owner who now ran it as a bed and breakfast.

The owner, Cassandra Riley, was most likely the woman on the porch. She was in her mid-thirties, widowed, and the sole owner and operator of the Admiral's Arms. She lived there with her daughter, age six. Riley had been a cheerleader at the University of Ohio who finished up with a masters' degree in physical therapy. She came to work in the Virginia tidewater area in her mid-twenties and fell for a Navy pilot. They'd married and quickly had their daughter.

After a few more years of a happy marriage, the husband had flown his F/A-18 into a wavetop somewhere in the Atlantic, and she became eligible to join the sorority of naval aviation widows around Oceania Naval Air Station, south of the Navy's big Norfolk base. But instead of staying around the familiar society near the Navy base as many do, she moved herself and her child to Brewer. Here, she had run a successful bed and breakfast business for the last five years.

When he had heard her story in the briefing, Dugan wondered why she'd opted for an isolated place like Brewer. Maybe she was administering her own therapy. Maybe the summers were busy enough to keep the memories pushed away. But it must have been lonely out here when the winter winds blew off the bay and the business went dead. Heartbreak? Stubbornness? He knew from secondhand experience that the insurance payoff would have been pretty good, so it probably wasn't the money.

According to the Admiral's Arms website, guests enjoyed an unparalleled, panoramic view of the area, from the bay to the Potomac, a pleasant pastime for summertime guests looking to connect with the unspoiled bay.

Unfortunately, this description had recently appealed to the more unlawful elements of society looking for a quiet and scenic place to hide their boat and to commit mass murder. Several of the bastards were now terrorizing Ms. Riley. Dugan assumed her daughter was down with the other hostages on the point, since he saw no sign of a child at the house.

The time for terrorizing must be drawing to a close. Everything pointed to Cassandra Riley and the other townspeople of Brewer being unnecessary to the kidnappers after the Handy and the speedboat made their rendezvous. The question was whether Sal could get the cavalry up here in time to sort out the hostages, then whether the Navy could take down the Handy and the fast mover without provoking a nuclear explosion in the middle of the bay. But that was the Navy's problem; he had the hostages to worry about.

When the Zetas could use a bullet to silence Riley in a nanosecond, her only hope for rescue was Dugan, lying uncomfortably cold and damp in the grass a hundred yards away and armed only with a gun optimized for short-range killing.

But whatever the priorities were of the crowd on the porch, Dugan sensed Riley was not one at the moment. After a few more orders, the boss and two members climbed in an SUV, leaving the second in command and two of the baseball hats on the porch with the Riley woman.

The big man settled into the shotgun seat, still hammering out orders in rapid-fire Spanish. The SUV sped off, disappearing down the lane, heading toward the town.

I'll see him later, Dugan thought.

One baseball hat wearer hesitated, then turned to look up the slope, giving Dugan a bad moment, until the punk hawked and spat in the grass. He had a hard face, flat nose, and cold eyes. Not the kind of person you'd want to leave your wife or daughter alone with. Riley continued to stand apart, arms folded protectively across her chest, looking off into the distance to Dugan's right, seeming to will a barrier between her and the nightmare that had descended on her quiet world.

As Guzmann's SUV disappeared, one man remaining on the porch made a remark, too low to be distinct, and the others laughed. Loudly.

Riley started for the door. One of them grabbed her wrist. The straw boss said something explosive in Spanish, and the thug dropped his hand. Riley disappeared into the house, briefly leaving the three on the porch before they filed through the door and out of sight.

Dugan realized that he'd been tense. He took a few deep breaths, letting them out slowly, and fought the impulse to go down to the house and start taking things apart. Too much was at stake. These were stone-cold killers, and they were playing with Riley like a cat plays with a mouse until he gets tired of the game.

The question was time, and Dugan's gut told him there wasn't much of it left. Hopefully the boss's instructions would keep Riley and her kid alive for a little longer. *But we're all on a clock, and the time we have is running out.* He had to get away, confirm the plan, and call for help, in that order.

Chapter 17

Getting away was easier. Instead of going back to the car in a straight line—following another rule drummed in by hard experience—Dugan dropped off the hillside to the west and made a big sweep around to the south. Once certain he was past the belt of cameras and motion detectors, he quickly worked his way back to the car. When he saw the shine of its bumper, he settled down behind a clump of vines and waited, testing the air for sounds, moving his head slowly back and forth, lips parted.

He waited a long ten minutes. The rain began again, and the wind picked up. Finally, knees protesting at a crouch held too long, Dugan made a wide circle around the car, taking his time, stepping carefully, until satisfied nobody waited in ambush. Approaching the car on the driver's side, he looked it over for signs of disturbance. The leaf telltales were still in place on the trunk lid, doors, and hood, and the door was solidly shut.

Noticing a loose door had saved his life once. Thanks to a man who years before, had taught him to put telltales in car doors, he had found a bomb hidden under a rental car's floormat. Later, Dugan passed on the lesson, with extra credit, to the Croatian who put the bomb in the car.

Dugan popped the trunk and stripped off the wet wool jacket and gloves, leaving him in the damp wool shirt and black stocking cap. He kicked off his boots, then hopped around on one leg at a time to strip off the soaking jeans, throwing them into the trunk. Finally, Dugan pulled the cap off his head, pressed it with his thumb and tossed it into the trunk. The white dot disappeared from the screens at Langley.

Before dropping the trunk lid, he pulled out an expensive camera bag, a small black nylon backpack, and his old brown leather jacket. Climbing into the car, he pulled out dry jeans from the clothes bag along with dry socks. He grimaced as he realized he would just have to put up with wet boots, but the dry wool socks helped.

While he dressed, Dugan debated his next move. His plans didn't call for armament, so the pistol went back into its hideaway. He looked briefly at the cell phone and saw a strong signal, but it would be from the makeshift cell tower put up by his opponents, not one he could safely use. He put the cell phone in the compartment with the pistol and slid the cover closed, then replaced the floormat.

He opened the car's glove compartment and took out the used leather wallet that held some cash, a Virginia driver's license in the name of Frank Simpson of Culpepper, Virginia, his credit cards, a voter registration card, and a picture of a little girl—his daughter, if anyone asked. Frank Simpson was a solid citizen of the Commonwealth, out for a weekend to take pictures of wildlife.

Dugan knew there actually *was* a Frank Simpson in the Culpepper phone book, just in case prying eyes ever got interested. But it was one of the trapdoors people in another agency maintained around the country. The lady's voice that answered the phone would be Simpson's wife, southern and courteous, engaging the caller in polite and prolonged conversation about Frank's photography obsession while the caller's location was plotted, and the posse started his way.

Dugan left the little knife in its sheath strapped to his leg. It wasn't the kind of thing Frank Simpson would wear, but Dugan knew if the opposition got around to looking inside his pants leg, old Frank would already be in a lot of trouble anyway.

Finally, he took a deep breath and turned the key in the switch. The engine started without blowing up—always a sign of progress, in his mind—and no goon squad ambushed him. Suddenly in a hurry to be out of there, he backed the car around on the pine needles and sandy soil and drove back down the muddy little lane to the highway. He hit the pavement, turning left toward town. The roads were still empty, and the rain lashed down on the highway. He reached down to crank up the heat, and the sudden blast of air warmed him.

The day was getting on. Even through the overcast skies, Dugan could tell the sun was approaching midafternoon, and he felt the increasing pressure of time in the back of his mind while he dealt with more immediate problems. The deserted two-lane he was on would take him from the south into Brewer. The town was half a mile away with the low ridge and the Admiral's Arms on the right.

There was no reason for him to spend any more time on the Riley house now that he knew where Guzmann and some of his thugs were keeping themselves. He still needed to know more about the layout in town.

But instead, he was planning on driving right up to the Admiral's Arms, right into the crosshairs like some lost tourist. A move like that would be reckless and probably would break a dozen tradecraft rules, all starting with "unnecessarily."

Sal would have a kitten, Dugan thought. *No, Sal would do more than disapprove; he would probably put me to teaching elementary field sanitation to trainees on the Farm.* But there was something about that lonely woman in the houseful of thugs that had gotten his attention and a closer look at the opposition wouldn't hurt either. When he came to the tasteful sign for the Admiral's Arms, he turned off the pavement to the right, down the gravel driveway toward the house.

The narrow road wound between old oaks and tangled underbrush. In the summer, the driveway would have been tree-shaded and evocative of older times in Virginia. In the winter though, the trees were dark and stripped of their leaves, reaching overhead in a vaguely menacing way. The road was smooth, and even with the occasional mudhole, it was well maintained. A good mark for Riley. The woman had run a successful business for herself, though now she had other concerns.

When Dugan's car emerged from the trees into the open, he pulled up behind the black four-wheel and killed the engine. There was no reaction from the house; no faces in the windows, no friendly wave, but no gunfire either, which he decided was a plus. He opened the door and was grabbing the camera case by its straps when Cassandra Riley walked onto the porch. She didn't look happy.

He got out of the car in a hurry, like a man would do in a rainstorm, and bounced up the steps. Riley was standing at the edge of the porch, blocking Dugan's way like someone who wanted to discourage visitors, but his quick, heads-down approach backed her up until they were both standing on the wide, covered porch. He positioned his body, so she had her back to the door while he faced the house.

Up close, she looked younger than he expected. Her reddish-brown hair was pulled back in a messy bun, and her blue eyes looked out from the creamy complexion that comes with redheads in the family line. Her white blouse and dark slacks more than hinted at a shapely figure. She wore no makeup, her eyes were rimmed with red, and she was straining to look normal. Dugan hoped his turn into her driveway didn't make things worse, though he doubted she could be worse off than she was now.

94

What she saw on her front porch, he hoped, was just a passing tourist. Dugan had spent a good part of his life trying to look so normal that unfriendly eyes would pass on by. With his medium-cut brown hair, brown eyes, and nondescript clothes, he was easily overlooked. He couldn't hide his 6'2" frame, but he tended to skinniness rather than muscle and had learned the art of hunching up to look shorter and less menacing. He smiled in a friendly way at Cassandra Riley and kept his hands in plain sight.

"Good morning," he said cheerfully. "I guess this is the Admiral's Arms?"

"Yes," she said, uncertainly. "But I'm sorry, we're…"

He held up one hand. "…not taking people who wander in with no reservations," he finished. Indicating the other car, he went on. "I know you're busy."

During the opening gambit he kept his eyes on her, but his real attention was on the door and the corners of the house. He guessed that with only the low-ranking punks here, they'd not know how to react, and he could keep them off-balance. If he was wrong though, a lot of timetables would be disrupted, and people would die in Riley's living room. But Dugan's blood was up; he could feel it. This woman and the others shouldn't be victims of such scumbags. So, he broke the rules and went into trouble the way Sal knew he would. That's why he stayed in the field while Sal went on to Langley.

"Well, we do have guests…" she said, still uncertain. The dark circles under her eyes stood out against her pale skin. Over her shoulder, Dugan could see a dark figure far back from the window. "I mean, we don't have any rooms…"

"I'm just passing through, and I don't need a room now. But in the spring, I'll be back for the wildlife. Birds, in fact. I take pictures." By now he was giving her all the charm he had, and she backed up like he had plague.

Dugan saw her fear. She'd been through so much lately that one more guy was another threat, a complication, not a rescue. With a house full of thugs, a single stranger didn't seem to be much help. Part of Dugan wanted to grab her and make for the car, but that was an obvious impossibility for a lot of reasons.

"I'll be through here later," he said, using his soft Shenandoah Valley accent, "following the spring migration north, and I hoped to spend some time in the area." She looked at him like he'd grown another head, so he kept babbling. "Lots of rare species come right through here. Species tough to find anyway. I'm looking for a place to stay, you know, and I saw your sign..."

"I'm sorry," she said, voice pitched higher. "I'm very busy. This is just a bad time. You'll have to excuse me." Her body language said plainly that if she could have thrown him bodily off the porch, she would.

As he was trying to think of some brilliant line that would give him a look inside, the door before him opened, and one of the thugs in a baseball cap appeared with a crooked smile on his face. Dugan was relieved to see his hands were empty.

"*Senora*," he said, looking at her with a smirky grin. "I think you should allow the *senor* a look around." Turning to Dugan he said, "*Buenos dias, Senor.* Please come in, *por favor.*" He held the door open and beckoned him inside, so in Dugan went.

As a general rule, Dugan had avoided being killed in his business by not doing dumb things. Deliberately going into that house was a really, really dumb thing, and every alarm bell in his head went off as he stepped into a large, pleasant sitting room with big glass windows overlooking the bay. The room was tastefully over-furnished, and the bric-a-brac scattered around looked as if it were from antique stores and estate sales.

The strong smell of stale maleness, sweat, unwashed bodies, and dirty linen attacked Dugan's senses. For a microsecond, he sensed the disorder, dirt, and menace beyond the front room.

Moving into the middle of the room, he sensed Riley behind him. The door was still open, the cold, clean air invading the room, but the tension was as thick as a bay fog. Dugan, playing his role as Frank Simpson from Culpepper, decided to back out fast.

"Say, this is great," he said. "But I can see you're busy with your, er, crew here."

The man from the porch stood with his heavily tattooed arms folded and a half-smirk that Dugan longed to wipe off the Latino's face. He had moved to one side of a doorway that opened to a long central hall. Dugan could see past him and had a glimpse of an empty room, with light streaming through open doors.

Cassandra Riley opened her mouth to say something when the other two men walked in, one through the front door behind Dugan and the other from the hallway.

Dugan took a casual shuffle step to the side, still rambling on about coming back in the spring. "I don't mean to intrude. I'll just be going now. I hope to see you again some time." With his step to the side, he had arranged Riley and the three goons into a loose circle in the large room. They hadn't liked it when he'd sidestepped, though Dugan had done it as Frank Simpson the tourist and not as a threat.

The hired help were off balance and wary. Their instructions hadn't covered a visiting *gringo,* particularly not a big one standing right here in the middle of the living room and talking a mile a minute.

For Dugan's part, he *was* Frank Simpson, amateur birder from the Shenandoah Valley, a harmless big man who was getting a little scared. For a second, Dugan's eyes met those of the one with the baseball hat, and he felt the menace in them like a blow. A challenge can pass between violent men in a half-instant, just like between animals, but the human reaction may be deadlier. Dugan had a lot of practice in looking meek, and Frank Simpson's eyes dropped before the thug could sense the murder in Dugan's thoughts. Like any wild animal, the bully felt a surge of superiority over this cowed tourist, a nonentity who could be frightened and dismissed.

The moment passed. The Latino was still off balance, but Dugan could see he was feeling more in control. His crew looked to him for instructions. If baseball-cap had been in charge, Dugan knew they would have tried to bring Frank Simpson down, but the *jefe* gave the orders, and the orders didn't cover Frank Simpson.

As he continued his act, Dugan could see the indecision on the thug's face and decided to give him some space to screen his departure, which was plainly in the cards. Clearly, Cassandra Riley could get no reassurances at this stage of their relationship. He'd seen what he needed to see. There was no sign of a six-year-old daughter, and Dugan really hadn't expected to see any. She was probably with the others while her home was used as a headquarters and her mother as a cook or worse.

Dugan estimated the odds against taking all these guys out now were too great, and a premature attack, successful or not, would disrupt a lot of other plans. Saving Riley would have to wait, he decided.

"Well," Simpson said, "like I was saying, didn't mean to intrude. I was passing by and thought I'd check out the place for later." He kept his hands by his sides, the camera dangling from his right hand. "I come down this way with my family sometimes and saw the sign." Anybody could tell that things weren't right, so he played out his role of a nervous bystander who scented trouble and wanted out.

The Latino's little eyes squinted as Dugan went through the Frank Simpson chatterbox routine. Dugan noticed the man looked twice at Dugan's soaked boots and his dry jeans. After a second, the man shrugged.

"Nice place here," he said. "The *senora* keeps it nice. We keep it up for her." This with a lift of his chin toward where Riley stood in the corner, arms folded across her chest, hugging herself. The others smiled.

"You come back in summer, man, be real good time." The creep leaning on the door snickered a little at that, which only increased Dugan's urge to move his nose to the other side of his face.

Well, there'll be a time for that, Dugan thought. He nodded, remembering to keep himself humble, and then turned to Cassandra Riley. "I'll do that, and thanks for letting me check out your place."

"Come back when you can," she said automatically as Dugan moved toward the door. The circles under her eyes spoke volumes.

He nodded, turning his back on them, and picked up a card from the table near the front door. Walking across the porch toward his car, he felt like he had a bullseye painted on his back. But he got to the car without incident, waved, and drove down the driveway. He watched the house through the rearview mirror, and just before he passed through the trees and out of sight, he saw three of the men start down the steps toward the SUV.

Well, sure.

Chapter 18

Wednesday 1500

One of the advantages Dugan had in dealing with people was that on a certain level, they were predictable. In a situation like this, there were typically two groups—a few professionals on the inside, and on the edges, a bunch of low-grade thugs preening, yanking out guns, and beating people up.

The first class of people was dangerous. Guzmann was a good example. He was an import from the Central American drug gangs, intelligence mixed with cunning, absolute ruthlessness, and enough muscle to be lifted out of run-of-the-mill stooge-dom.

In fact, Dugan knew from Sal's hasty pre-briefs that Guzmann operated on a high level for a criminal, coordinating with the Russian or Ukrainian mobs and with the people coming in on the ship. That was unusual enough, Dugan knew—the Russians or the Ukes normally don't open up to people outside their own clans—but it was really unusual that he was powerful enough to lead the European thugs alongside the Latinos and even more, to press a rough chain of command on them.

The money must be really good.

After Guzmann, the Europeans seemed to be in charge, judging from his encounter with the two would-be murderers and the patrol in the woods. The Latinos seemed to be the bigger crowd of low-class hoodlums who were doing the grunt work, like guarding the hostages in the house down on the water, looking after the cars, doing the feeding, and so forth.

Dugan could sense things beginning to move. The ship was just hours out. The thugs from the house were going to react to his visit, one way or another. Being the kind of bottom-feeders that Guzmann's local hires were, they were prone to violence as a first choice. Thinking came in second by a long shot. When someone poked a finger in their chest, it would take them a minute to realize they ought to be worried about the big Anglo who had just dropped in out of nowhere.

There was nothing to do now but play the ball where it lay. Dugan hit the highway and turned left toward Brewer. He knew the goons would be close behind. The downpour had eased off temporarily. The clouds might have been lifting, though the wind still whipped the bare branches on the oaks beside the road. As he drove, he tried to remember the wind limits for the drones and gave up.

He felt a twinge of worry. He needed to communicate soon, but if the opposition had a way to pinpoint calls, then turning on a phone would bring them down around his ears. But time was running out. His best option was to poke around for the next few hours and see what opened up. As he drove, his thoughts returned to the woman in the Admiral's Arms. Cassandra Riley and the old man from the house by the beach were on his mind, and a six-year-old kid whose kindergarten picture had looked out at him from a file folder during mission planning. These people had done nothing to deserve being near death.

~

Driving into Brewer was like coming into any one of a hundred small towns in this part of Virginia—a scattering of small, white-

101

frame houses on either side of the road, sometimes with a boat on a trailer in the driveway or on a rough cradle in the back yard. In the spring and summer, these houses would have flower beds and trimmed walks, while the men and women whose ancestors had lived on the same land would be up early and off to jobs at the county seat or motoring out to check the crab traps and pound nets.

Life moved at its own pace here, though the satellite television stations would bring their flicking colors and loud talk to living rooms and draw off the young ones to the cities. Some came back, but not enough to fill all the houses, and here and there, Dugan saw empty shells and blank windows set back from the road, just as he had seen on his way from Stafford.

He slowed as he closed on the town. Brewer opened in front of him as he came out of the woods in a gentle left-hand turn. The town was so small he could see all the way down the main street to where the road dead-ended at the old crab packing house and the piers on the water with a white workboat tied to the pilings at one of the piers.

There was a four-way intersection just short of the piers, where the paved roads ran along the waterfront. Dugan knew from studying the maps that the one to the right ran out to the point of land and the old house that had been the destination of his nocturnal swim. To the left, the road ran about a quarter of a mile, angling away from the water and eventually stopping at the town dump. Riley's bed and breakfast was a quarter of a mile away as the crow flies, through some trees and up a gentle slope.

As Dugan drove into town, he recalled what he had been briefed about Brewer. The water depth off the town pier was five and half feet at low tide. The town's only gas station had been built in 1978 and had a capacity for about five thousand gallons. One power line and one telephone cable connected the town to the rest of the world. Scarcely a hundred people listed Brewer as their home, and most of them lived in the country on the outskirts. The town had one working restaurant connected to the gas station and a bait shop open three days a week. That was it.

Just short of the four-way stop, he turned right into the dirt parking lot next to the filling station and killed the engine. Dugan wanted another cup of coffee and to hell with the consequences. Sal would disapprove, but Dugan could feel the devil rising in him again—the recklessness that was always there when people started pushing him around. It made him a bad covert agent, but Sal had put him on this mission anyway, maybe just because he knew Dugan was the way he was.

Inside the roadside shop, he thought he might find a cup of coffee. He might also find out a little more about what was going on in the town. Dugan took a deep breath to get the devils under control again and walked into the restaurant.

The layout was familiar to anyone who had eaten in a small-town diner. There was a glass counter with an old cash register on the right, a line of red-leatherette booths down each wall with the kitchen at the end. A door on the left opened into the filling station, and through the open door was another glass counter, dirtier and scarred with the clutter of the trade—fan belts, stacks of oilcans, old rags.

In a booth at the back of the restaurant, two men sat hunched over a table; the one facing the door looked up when Dugan walked in. He was a large man, with streaks of white in a short and ragged black beard. He wore a stained army field jacket, damp from the rain. The dirty baseball hat pushed back on his head had the horsehead patch of the Army's First Cavalry Division. Dugan could only see the back of the man's companion, but he looked to be younger, smaller, and just as work stained.

Dugan figured them to be the men who ran the filling station. He nodded, walked to a booth across from the entrance to the filling station, and sat down. There was a silence.

"You want something?" the older guy asked. His voice rumbled out like it came from deep in the ground. The way he said it was a challenge, not a question.

"Coffee."

"Pour it yourself. Dorothy ain't here this morning."

"Thanks," Dugan said, walking back to the coffee pot beside the door to the kitchen. He took a Styrofoam cup from the stack beside the pot and poured himself a cup. He looked at the filling station crew and raised the pot. The big guy shook his head, so Dugan returned the pot and went back to his seat facing the door. He didn't like having people behind him, but there wasn't much choice. He was expecting company, and he either faced the door with the big guy and his friend behind him or faced them with his back to the door. The door would be where the trouble came from.

The coffee tasted like tar. Old tar. Except for the two behind him, the place was as deserted as the town. Dugan sipped the bitter drink and pushed his back against the wall, sitting sideways so he could see the door and the two mechanics. His tail would be along in a minute, so he waited patiently.

The big guy kept looking at him. Finally, Dugan met his eyes. The Cavalryman's eyes were black and hostile, and this time Dugan didn't do his Frank Simpson fade. After a minute or two of locking eyes, the man had to speak.

"You passin' through?" he said.

"I'm just here to look at birds," Dugan said, sipping the coffee. Bitter and burned. Well, at least it was hot. "You a vet?"

"First Cav," he said. "Iraq." There was a silence.

"You really looking at birds?"

Dugan nodded and took a sip.

"You don't look like no birdwatcher," the vet said.

"How's a birdwatcher supposed to look?" Dugan said.

"Like I give a shit," the man said.

His smaller friend turned to look at Dugan from his seat. "No birds around here," the small man said.

Everybody was so damned unfriendly. They might have hurt Frank Simpson's feelings, Dugan thought.

"Plenty of birds, if you know where to look. You guys run the garage?"

"Yeah," said the veteran. "My place. Born right down the road." He looked at Dugan in a considering way, less hostile. "Where you from?"

"D.C.," Dugan said. The game was getting old. "Where the hell is everybody in this town?"

Dugan saw their jaws clamp down. They both looked at him straight and flat, and then without a word, turned back to whatever it was they had been doing before he came in. Dugan took a sip and would have tried to restart the conversation if he hadn't seen the SUV pull into the gravel parking lot outside the restaurant.

He walked to the coffee pot to refill his cup. The door slammed open and the baseball-cap Latino rushed in with two friends, one of them the blond European from the guard patrol this morning. In the nanosecond before action, Dugan was faintly surprised to see the European and decided he must have been in the back of the house all along.

The newcomers ignored the two men seated in the rear of the dining room and came straight for Dugan, and it wasn't to talk. With the layout of the restaurant, Dugan was trapped with two unknown civilians behind him and these creeps in front. Well, he'd asked for it.

Without hesitating or speaking, he threw the hot coffee pot at the nearest one, then charged the group before they could react. A knee to the groin of the first man doubled him over, and Dugan followed with a rising lefthanded punch to catch the European's chin that cracked his head back.

The thug who had been in the rear produced a nasty-looking baseball bat and chopped at Dugan, but the others were in the way and the blow went wild.

Amateurs. Dugan grabbed the bat as it went by and shoved it into the European's face with a satisfying crack. Dugan pushed him aside and went after the batsman with a straight right that caught his nose, knocking him against the glass counter.

Dugan heaved forward to untangle himself from the close quarters fight in the cramped restaurant. The thug who'd been kneed was bent over and out of action for a while, but the guy with the bat and the blond European straightened and started throwing punches, most of them wild. Dugan had little trouble slipping them. They were lousy hand-to-hand fighters, Dugan realized. These two were fighting like amateurs, pulling back and trying to hit with long-range punches. *Sad.*

Dugan closed in, hit the European with a cross-punch to the nose, and while he was trying to squint through the tears, Dugan chopped him with the heel of his hand, and he dropped... and then something hit Dugan hard from behind. Suddenly his cheek was against the gritty floor, and he was hearing sounds from far, far off while all he could see, through waves like heat rising from the floor, was shoes and boots dancing around in front of him. He blacked out.

Chapter 19

Wednesday 1600

"Baltimore pilot calling the motor vessel Arco Trader," the voice said on Channel 16, the international hailing channel. A minute later a similar call went out to the other ship.

As commercial vessels pass through the U.S. maritime security zones and approach the channels leading to American ports, they are required to pick up pilots to guide the ships from sea to port. In the case of the Chesapeake, channel pilots guide the ships from the sea to the port entrances in Norfolk or Baltimore, then the ship is handed over to local harbor pilots for the actual dockage.

Pilots, tugboat crews, stevedores, deep-water fishermen, and others who operate in America's seaports and harbors make up a class of professionals and tradesmen who are generally overlooked by the greater population inland, but they are essential to the nation's economic success. As a class they are experienced and highly competent at their often-risky jobs. The maritime professions in the Norfolk, Virginia area contain a high proportion of former and retired Navy and Coast Guard veterans who run their businesses in the sea services' shipshape manner. They are fiercely patriotic. Even at this short notice, it wasn't hard at all to sell Sal's plan to the crews of the pilot boats. They also understood the need for secrecy.

In the Langley operations center, an airman turned to the Air Force general. "They're calling the ships, sir," she said.

The general turned to Sal. "I heard," he said.

~

Dugan first became aware that he was freezing. And then pain, a lot of it. He was lying in a dark, cold tunnel with a light at the end. Sometimes the light would get close, and then it would be far away. He was getting colder, so the next time the light came close, he held onto it with his eyes and swam toward it. It was daylight.

Except this daylight came faintly in through a dirty window high up on a cinderblock wall, and after a moment, Dugan could hear the sound of rain beating on it. Hard. He focused on the wall. After a minute passed and his head began to clear, he realized he was lying on a smelly, lumpy mattress. He moved his arm to touch his head, and his hand came back sticky.

So don't put your hand up there, he thought, cautiously moving his arms and legs. They seemed to be attached and answering his brain. He rolled to the side of the mattress, smelling its musty, earthy odor, and got his knees under him. For a moment, that was enough. For long seconds, he knelt there gathering his strength, feeling the nausea that comes with a head wound. He was just starting to stand when the door opened, and the First Cavalry veteran walked in carrying an unlit kerosene space heater.

"You're finally awake," he observed without emotion. "Thought your head was busted wide open."

"Not dead yet." Dugan's mouth wasn't working quite right, and the words came out slurred.

"So I see," the veteran said. "Glad of that, I guess." He put the heater down, turned a knob, and clicked the starter until the burner caught. Dugan could feel the heat from the little tongues of blue flame and was grateful for their warmth. He sat heavily on the mattress, and the big man moved the heater closer to him. Dim light flooded the little room.

"You took a pretty good whack," the man said. "Thought you'd had it. But they just kept beatin' on you."

Dugan's eyes were gradually focusing, and he looked around the dim room. *Cinderblock walls and rough, empty shelves. The dirty window with the splatters of rain. Some kind of storeroom then.*

The door was still open, and through it, in the dim light of the kerosene heater, Dugan glimpsed another, larger room. Muddled sounds came from it. He remembered there had been two men in the restaurant before the arrival of the posse. Through the door, he could barely make out a dusty window in the other room.

From the dim light, he realized it must be late afternoon. Hours had passed. The thought snapped him awake. He pressed the illumination button on his cheap black watch and shivered. Four hours had gone by. Enough time left, but just enough.

"You didn't look like no civilian," the larger man said. "Deion and me, we took a chance when they was working on you. Had a couple of tire irons from the shop, so while they were beatin' on you, we did some beatin' ourselves," he said with a satisfied air.

As if on cue, the smaller man stuck his head around the corner from the other room. He grinned. "Deion, that be me, and we got all three of your dancin' partners in here, a couple all hanked up. The other one's not going to be making trouble ever." He took a deep breath.

Dugan got to his feet, took a step, swayed a little, then felt the ker-thunk that came when all his parts started working together. The nausea receded. He walked to the other room and saw the thug who had been swinging the bat and the European, both trussed like pigs and gagged for good measure, with a few assorted bruises and skinned places thrown in.

In a corner, the third one lay in a shapeless pile. The head and face were bloody and misshapen. Dugan looked back at the veteran and got a flat stare back in the gloom.

"I can't just call you 'big guy'," Dugan said.

"Jonah," he said. "Miller. You got beat up in my gas station. And don't buy that jive-talk shit from Deion. He's the only genuwine college grad-u-ate that the big city of Brewer ever produced." He pronounced it PRO-duced.

"I bet you know we got trouble," he continued. "Leastwise, I'll tell you we got trouble. We took a chance on you, mister, and if we're wrong, we just killed more people than that one asshole in there." He took a deep breath. "I done some killin' in the war, but this is my hometown, and beatin' a guy's head in in my own garage is tough shit, man. So just who the hell are you, mister, and what the hell is going on?"

Dugan didn't hesitate. He saw no reason to hold back from them at this point, so for the first time in his professional life, he told the truth. Or part of it.

"I'm Neil Dugan. I'm an agent of the U.S. government, and I'm going to need your help."

Deion leaned on the jamb within view of the two tied-up in the other room. Both men looked at Dugan and waited.

"What happened after I blacked out?" Dugan asked.

"Deion and me, we waded in with tire irons. They were so busy with you, they never saw us comin'."

"Where's their SUV?"

"Deion hid it in the garage. Locked the doors all around."

"Where's that Ford I drove in?" Dugan asked.

"Still parked back at the station," said Jonah. "But mister, I wouldn't be goin' back there. Cleaned up the place, wiped up the blood and stuff. But sooner or later they goin' to be all over town, trying to figure out where these three went and where we are."

110

Dugan wasn't sure that would be the case. Darkness was coming, and the other side had a tight timetable. But he had to admit, not going out in the open made a lot of sense.

"Where are we?" he asked. "How far are we from town?"

"Think we could move all you people that far?" Jonah asked. "We're in the old crab packin' house. Downtown at the end of the road. We mostly carried you and dragged them, and we had to go quick. Kept behind the buildings, came in on the dock side."

Dugan did some arithmetic in his head. Counting the guards at the old mansion and two or three at Riley's place, his opponents probably wouldn't be able to free up enough people for a real search. They were as pressed for time as Sal and Dugan were, for different reasons. He guessed that if they searched at all, it would be perfunctory, and then they would wonder what the hell was going on and where the three had taken off to, but they would try to stay on the timeline.

The lower-ranking hoods might not even tell Guzmann their pals had disappeared. If what Dugan had heard was true, Guzmann did not encourage freelancing or deviations from his plans, and he had been known to shoot the messenger bearing bad news.

"Do you guys have any guns?" Dugan asked.

They both smiled. "Assholes came in, took everybody's car keys and guns," Jonah said. "They think they got everything."

Deion walked over to a dusty cupboard and pulled out two pump shotguns that looked to be 12-gauge. Jonah took one, and in his hands, it looked tiny. "Few boxes of shells, too. Hid these out down here right after they came."

"Got these of'n these assholes," he added, pulling out a black pistol from his back pocket, another from an old blanket piled up on the floor, and two extra clips. Deion grinned and pulled out a Glock.

Dugan picked up one of the Berettas and pulled the slide back. It was the standard 9mm, like the one he had found earlier in the would-be killers' SUV.

God, was that just this morning? he thought. There was a round already up the spout. He let the slide go forward and set the safety. It was a small arsenal, and he felt better already—the dead man next door and his aching head notwithstanding.

"These guys have any phones on them?" he asked.

Jonah dug into his pockets. He came out with two cheap cell phones. "They had these, man. I was gonna call for help but service out here is the pits."

Relief ran through Dugan's body. "Not just the pits. These bastards would've been on your heads in ten minutes. They've got their own cell system and can track locations on these phones."

Jonah grunted, and Dugan checked each phone for battery life, then crammed them both in his pockets.

Outside it was getting darker. Not time yet, he figured, but close.

"How did they do it?" he asked. "How'd they round up a whole town?"

"Not hard," Jonah said. "Must not be forty people in town during daytimes. They came in vans, spread out around town, then pulled guns and rounded everybody up at my station. Did a lot of pushin' and yellin'." He spat out the door in the general direction of their tied-up guests.

"Bill Harker and Jake Lee told 'em to go to hell and started swinging. They beat Bill and Jake up pretty bad." He paused. "I don't know if they're still 'live. After, they went door-to-door outside town, some of the farms close to town. Got about a hundred folks. Then they tied ever'body together and walked 'em down to the old Walker place."

"Why the Walker place?"

"House is big enough for ever'body, set away from town. They left us two in town just to make it seem natural. Left the telephone lines in the houses, so's the phone company won't get an error signal. Nobody around to answer the phones anyway. It's been about three days now. They go out and get food now and then."

"They tellin' us they're gonna leave, and nobody will get hurt," Deion said.

"But, mister, my mom and dad are over there, and unless we do something, I don't think they're ever gonna be turned loose," Jonah said.

Deion grimly nodded. "My wife and kid, and my parents too," he said, and Dugan noticed the country-boy accent fading away.

"The guys who have you are part of a Central American drug gang," Dugan said. "Seriously bad people." He wondered how much to tell them. These two deserved at least a little more honesty, he thought. "We know there's a ship coming in through the capes tonight, destination Baltimore."

Dugan paused, gathering his thoughts, making the lie easier for them to believe. "Sometime late tonight, it'll pass Smith Point Light, out where the Potomac meets the Chesapeake."

Both men nodded. They knew the bay much better than he did.

"The Feds think the freighter will drop a huge haul of pure cocaine into the water," Dugan said. "Straight from Colombia. The people who are holding your folks are part of the cartel moving it up here. They've got a go-fast in the old Walker boathouse they're planning to use to meet the freighter and tow the bundles to shore."

Dugan studied their faces to see if they believed him.

"To make all this work, they needed a place near the mouth of the river where they could wait to meet the boat. Then a place where they could haul the stuff ashore and break it into travel-sized bundles. It'll probably take them a few days."

"If the Feds know they're here, why don't they come get them?" Deion asked.

"That's why I'm here," Dugan said. "To find out where they are so we can take them down."

"Why take all the people? Gangs move drugs all the time," Jonah said.

"The stakes here are huge," Dugan said. "If this load gets on shore and makes it to market, it will transform the drug business on the east coast." He paused again. "It's so big that the lives of a hundred people in this town won't matter a damn."

Actually, Dugan was a little surprised that they were still alive. It was a major hole in the logic considering these people were totally ruthless, completely without feeling. Dugan figured that as long as the hostages lived, the gang's hold on Jonah and Deion preserved the appearance of daily life they needed in Brewer. And massacring over a hundred people in cold blood was a big step, even for Zetas, unless thousands more were dead as well. After the rendezvous with the ship, nobody on shore would be needed anymore, and anyone left alive was a liability.

"So what are we goin' to do?" asked Jonah, who was also losing his country-boy accent.

Dugan noticed Deion holding back a little. *He didn't buy the whole story,* Dugan thought. But he needed help from these men, and he *wanted* to help them. *So much for professional detachment,* he thought. He could feel the Black Dog coming on again, the recklessness and urge for action that held him in the field for so long. Anger surged through his body and flushed his face as the two men stood looking at him. He paused a brief second to calm down. These men had risked their necks for him, gambled their lives, and for all they knew, the lives of their families. They needed him now. There was a lot to do, and time was running out.

"It's not as bad as it sounds," he said. "I'm not the only one around." He took another five minutes to explain what he meant and what they had to do. Outside, Dugan heard the wind gusting up again, and the rain beating hard on the windows. It was going to be a cold, dirty night.

Chapter 20

Wednesday 1800

As Dugan explained himself to Jonah and Deion, two gray pilot boats put off from Lynnhaven Inlet on the Atlantic shore and began to shoulder their way through the whitecaps. Each boat was built strong. The steel decks were broad and flat, the windscreens were tough, thick, no-shatter Plexiglas. The pilot-style seats inside featured lap and chest straps that gripped their occupants like astronauts. The straps were necessary because pilots boarded ships in all weathers, and the boats often took fearful poundings from the big Atlantic waves that built up coming over the continental shelf.

Below, they were basically seagoing power plants. The hulls were built around two huge 4000hp Caterpillar diesels, and the boats slammed their way through the storm with power to spare, pitching in the chop, tossing white spray to the side while their passengers and crew were thrown against the straps and absorbed the shocks.

In each boat, waiting to climb the accommodation ladder to his assigned ship's bridge, sat a man in sea boots, foul-weather bibbed trousers, and a red parka with built-in buoyancy. Each wore a baseball cap cocked back on his head and an orange inflatable life jacket around his neck with "Pilot" stenciled on the left side. On his person and in his pack, he carried the right credentials.

But unseen beneath the bulky clothing that could be expected in these conditions, each man wore a skin-tight rubberized diver's suit with a thin layer of high-tech insulation and a one-way valve to expel sweat and heat buildup. The two men were Navy SEALs, and they were risking their lives to pass as legitimate bay pilots.

Their mission was to board the two ships and identify which carried a deadly cargo. Each man was a volunteer, and each was completely confident he would survive. And, from repeated missions in the Middle East, each spoke conversational Arabic.

Even in calm weather, transferring pilots at sea looks, to a novice, like a collision between the moving ship and the pilot boat. The pilot boat must jam its rubberized bow rails against the ship's plates under full power while the ship looms above. While the two hulls grate together, the pilot makes his way along the deck handrails until he or a crewman can grasp the boarding ladder let down from the ship's main deck, often forty feet above the surface.

A sailor on the ship drops a light heaving line, to which the crewman on the pilot boat clips the pilot's small boarding pack, and it's hoisted aloft. Then the pilot climbs up the dizzily swaying ladder to the deck, while the pilot boat pulls away and leaves nothing beneath the transferring pilot but the heaving sea. It has been done this way for hundreds of years.

Each SEAL was in magnificent physical shape. The climb was simple, though to avoid suspicion, they took their time. Pilots are usually men well into middle age, and this would be an arduous climb under the circumstances of the weather and heavy sea. A reception committee of bundled-up sailors and one officer met each man, shook his hand, and courteously took him to the bridge to meet the captain.

Chapter 21

Wednesday 1830

Dugan was tired. He felt his age, and though he was in superb shape, he could feel the aftereffects of swimming all night and then playing in the woods all morning, not to mention getting knocked around after lunch. *And no lunch, come to think of it.*

Darkness would come early in this season. It was past the solstice, and the days were getting longer, but daylight still went away early, with the heavy cloud cover hastening the darkness. Dugan felt in his pocket for one of the two phones, flipped open the clamshell cover, and studied the phone's face while he thought.

Sal needs some kind of signal. Gambling that the temporary system set up by the gang wasn't good enough to get a fix on a position burst, Dugan dialed Sal's private number, listened to the rings, and hung up after two. It was a private signal they had used before in other places.

~

At the Langley operations center, Sal's private cell phone buzzed. He didn't recognize the number of the incoming call. The phone rang a second time and then fell silent. A smile flickered across his impassive face.

The Air Force general walked over, drawn by Sal's concentration and the fleeting expression on his face.

Sal held up the phone. "There he is. Nobody else has my number. He's not on his normal cell phone, but he's telling us he's okay. We'll get the full story later, but for now, get the word out."

The general turned to his staff officers, and Sal picked up the direct line to the Situation Room.

~

While Dugan and his new allies waited for full darkness, Jonah snuck back to the restaurant and came back with packaged sandwiches, crackers, and beer. The three men mumbled a little as they ate, but they were mostly silent, thinking about the night ahead. Dugan noticed Deion would stir every now and then, as if he wanted to talk. But then he would look at Jonah, take his cue from the big silent man, and just sit staring at the walls, chewing his sandwich.

Dugan checked on the two prisoners. They were conscious but quiet, testing their knots, straining against the ropes that bound them. With Deion covering him, Dugan checked their knots himself and tugged the ropes, looking for slack. The Jonah/Deion team had been thorough, and there were no major adjustments to make.

Dugan didn't waste time asking questions. He believed the blond European was an imported professional and questioning him and the other one would make noise and distract them from their urgent tasks this night. So the three men just sipped their beer, chewed their sandwiches, and watched the bound men.

~

The two ships neared the Baltimore channel piloted by the disguised SEALs. Once past the narrow entrance through the Chesapeake Bay Bridge-Tunnel, the bay itself was so broad and so well marked that the SEALs could play their roles without endangering the ships they boarded. The only barrier was the gap in the bridge-tunnel, and before the mission, each SEAL got a crash course from a real pilot on navigating the narrow opening. As a result, both ships successfully passed the bridge-tunnel by putting on more power than usual to negate the effect of tidal currents in the opening, then reducing power once the bridge had been passed.

On the bridge of the lead ship, the SEAL kept up his nautical chatter as he watched the GPS screen and the ship's course. He was a big, breezy guy, a natural actor, and he behaved as he thought a local pilot should, down to a Tidewater accent, figuring that if the middle eastern officers on the bridge thought him a chatty, light type, that would be better for his deadly serious mission.

The ship's officers were careless with what they said in their native tongue within his hearing. In minutes, he was sure he had boarded the target ship. As darkness fell and the Handy passed into the bay, it reduced speed and began to plow down the long and straight Baltimore Channel. The pilot excused himself from the bridge to answer a call of nature. With a nod from the officer of the deck, two members of the bridge crew followed him out of the pilot house, drawing their pistols as they left.

The SEAL sensed his followers as he left the bridge. The two men rushed to keep up with him as he bounded down the ship's ladder to the second deck and disappeared. In the darkness through the rain, they dashed with drawn pistols toward where they supposed he would be.

Before they could fully grasp what was happening, the SEAL stepped from behind a bulwark, chopped their gun hands down, and smashed their heads together. Then in a single movement, the SEAL vaulted over the rail into the tossing, black waves far below. When he surfaced, he swam away from the ship's propeller with powerful backstrokes.

Dazed, the two pursuers scrambled for their pistols and fired wildly into the receding waves. After a moment, by unspoken consent, they climbed the ladder to the bridge and reported a fight to the death on the second deck, after which they threw the infidel's body into the sea. No one questioned them.

Half a mile behind, the SEAL lay relaxed in the waves like his animal namesake, held afloat by his inflated flotation collar and his dry suit. He turned his body slightly to the northeast to better ride the wave patterns and called his control on his miniature very high frequency radio. Then he relaxed in the waves and activated his beacon for the pickup.

On board the second ship, the SEAL was by now positive his ship was *not* the target they sought. As if reading his thoughts, his pocket communicator vibrated against his leg, and with a look of apology at the Spanish captain, the SEAL held the phone to his ear, nodded, and then asked a crewman for his boarding pack. When it was produced, the SEAL reached into a concealed pocket and brought out an impressive official-looking folio with a badge and identity card.

"Captain," he said with as much official urgency as he could put in his voice. "I have to inform you that I am an official of the U.S. Coast Guard, and I order you to observe radio silence, stop this vessel immediately, and come to anchor."

The mystified captain opened his mouth to protest, but the SEAL held up his hand. "This involves the security of the United States, of your crew, and this ship. Failure to follow my instructions will result in heavy fines and probably jail time for you and your mate. A Coast Guard vessel will be alongside in minutes. I must insist that you anchor, and above all, not use the radio."

The captain did not anchor, but he did order the engine room to reduce speed to the minimum required to keep the ship under control.

Minutes later, the officers of the ship assembled on the bridge facing the SEAL, who stood unmoving and only repeated his orders. After a tense five minutes, the impasse broke when a 45-foot Coast

Guard Medium Response Boat came into view with the first SEAL aboard. A genuine Coast Guard officer took charge and reinforced the SEAL's orders. Within minutes, the *Arco Trader*'s anchor buried itself in the soft mud at the bottom of the bay. There were no radio calls.

The first ship, the Handy, sailed on unknowingly.

~

The flat screens in the Langley operations center still showed nothing but thick cloud over the two ships when the SEAL report came in. Sal smiled a humorless smile. *Bingo. The target is verified. Always better to have a man at the scene.* He reached for the phone to the White House situation room.

Chapter 22

Wednesday 2000

Dugan was uneasy about what would be happening at the Admiral's Arms after nightfall, so he pushed the timeline a little. When it was dark, he turned to Deion. "You in good shape? Like, can you run?"

"Yeah, man," he whispered in reply. "What you got in mind?"

"Something dangerous." He took a cell phone out of his pocket and checked to make sure the battery was still charged. It was. He turned it off quickly and looked at Deion.

"You're going to call the cavalry to come rescue us, and it's probably the most dangerous thing we're going to do tonight."

Deion crossed his arms and set his jaw in determination.

"The people running this thing have set up their own cell phone net and can track calls in a New York minute. The bastards closed in on me fast this morning. We have to assume they can still do it, and in fact, they're probably a little more nervous now than before. But we've got to get word out to start the evening's festivities."

Dugan handed Deion the phone. "I want you to get as far from town as you can in thirty minutes. That means running. And you need to stay away from roads. Call the number I'm going to give you, pass a message, and run like hell back here. Make sure you shut off the phone before you start coming back."

Dugan could feel the man's intensity in the dark. "This call is the secret to our success and the way we get your family back. I know it's pouring, but you need to keep the phone as dry as possible."

Deion nodded in the gloom.

"If you don't get a signal on this phone or if it doesn't work, here's the backup." He pulled out the second disposable phone taken from the trussed-up prisoners and went through the same battery check.

"You're going to use the phone to call a guy named Sal," Dugan explained to Deion. "Talk only to him. I'm ninety-nine percent sure he'll be the one who answers. If somebody else picks up, insist on talking just to Sal." Dugan did not want some staffer blowing off Deion's message.

"He may ask you a question or two to verify who you are. If that happens, tell him that Neil sent you and tell him what's going on. Don't take too long, because the goons are tracking the signal. Tell Sal it's time. Just that. It's time. He knows what to do after that. Anybody got a paper and pencil? And we're going to need a plastic bag, too."

After a few heartbeats, Jonah and Deion realized Dugan was serious, and Jonah snuck back to the filling station to get the things they needed. Dugan believed it was worth the wait. Their lives depended on getting these calls through, and Dugan didn't want Deion, college education or not, standing out there in the dark after a thirty-minute run trying to remember if the critical number ended in a six or a nine.

Assuming he could get onto the porch of a house or under something to shelter from the rain, Deion could use the light from the little screen to double-check his numbers. Dugan wrote out the phone number, then Deion rolled it up with the phones in the shopping bag. They went over the call procedures one more time, including the part about running back.

"I'm going for the lady from the Admiral's Arms. I'll have her here by the time you get back. You'll wait with her for the law."

Deion nodded, and Dugan saw his teeth flash in the dark. Deion was already armed with the Glock, so without another word, he bumped fists with Jonah and slipped out the door into the storm. Dugan guessed he would ease through town and then take off down one of the dirt side roads. He hoped the cell phones would stay dry long enough to get the call through on one phone or another. Hopefully the opposition would be focused at the Walker house without enough manpower or inclination for foot patrols around town.

Then it was Dugan's turn to go. He waited a few minutes to make sure Deion was away, then he slipped outside into the rain and eased around the back of the old crab house, a 9mm stuck in his back pocket with a round in the chamber, the little knife still on his leg. The dock and waterfront were directly behind him. Moving cautiously, he crept slowly from behind the building toward another to his right and from there to another.

The wind blew harder from the northeast, and the rain still slanted down. Without a hat, the rain beat into his face, and he wiped his eyes with his forearm. *I should have borrowed Jonah's hat,* he thought too late. The clouds were heavy and low, which he suspected cut out the low-altitude drones and all but the most powerful infrared. It looked to be a nasty night.

The rain cut down visibility, so once away from the crossroads in the center of town, he moved more easily, just off the shoulder of the dead-end road that ended at the dump, stumbling a little when the ground got uneven. He saw no movement. Jonah had said the thugs left a few lights on in town to keep up appearances, but none of them were close enough to expose him.

Once he'd cleared the buildings in the town, Dugan moved into the open and started walking fast. The time for sneaking around was almost at an end, and he was betting the rain and sleet covered his movement. He had no technology to help this time—no GPS, not even an old-fashioned compass, but Dugan believed he wouldn't need one tonight. The navigation problem was pretty simple. Stay along the shore as the road veered toward the dump until the ground rose on the left, go through the trees, find the dock, and go uphill to the Admiral's Arms.

Dugan needed to free Riley before Guzmann's thugs killed her. He figured she was still alive only because Guzmann wanted to live in comfort at the Admiral's Arms, separating himself from the rest of the gang as a true *caudillo* should. But her lease on life was running out fast. Once the ship arrived and Guzmann turned over the go-fast to the people onboard, he didn't need the Admiral's Arms, Cassandra Riley, or any of the others.

Working time and distance calculations in one part of his mind as he moved through the rainy dark, he figured he had about two hours before things would speed up down at the house by the water. He felt the pressure of the little knife on his leg. The Velcro sheath had stayed put through everything, and as he moved through the freezing rain, he decided some guy in a Langley laboratory was going to get a case of *cerveza* from him when this was over.

Chapter 23

Wednesday 2030

The clouds almost completely cut out the infrared from the unmanned sensors, but the cover thinned momentarily and an alert operator at Langley got a screen capture of a little glowing dot moving south and east out of town. Another heat signature moved along the margin of the bay, heading north toward the Admiral's Arms.

Sal's arms were folded across his chest, his face impassive. For hours, no signal had come except the brief ring, and now the experiences of thirty-four years of covert operations and Sal's history with Dugan were stretching to understand what the glowing dots meant. With a nod to the Air Force general, the picture on the big screen switched out toward the bay and the Baltimore channel.

Sal and the general watched the intermittent signatures that indicated much larger objects moving toward the junction of the bay and the Potomac. Sal was still there, unmoving, watching the movement of the ships when his private cell phone rang.

~

Dugan left the road when it veered away from the water and the high ground rose on the left. He once again paralleled the shore, moving up the slope through trees and thickets, bulling his way through the knee-high grasses and small shrubs. The rain fell hard, and he repeatedly wiped his eyes to pick out a path in the rough, muddy terrain. The wind was strong enough to push him hard, and he knew that if he stopped, he would freeze.

His eyes adjusted, but it was still dark enough in the weeds and under the shrubs to hide the folds in the ground. He stumbled frequently as he moved across the broken terrain with one arm in front of his face to protect his eyes. He sensed occasional patches of open water on his right, then stumbled across a path that led downhill along the shore through the cattails and other sea grasses. Moving more cautiously on the trail, Dugan began to close in on where he thought the dock should be, with its path up the hill to the inn.

The trail suddenly opened, and he knew he was emerging from the brush onto the house's broad, open lawn. High up on his left, car lights swept across the sky, moving along the circular driveway.

Some of the boys leaving, he thought. He got his bearings. *So the house is ... there... and the dock should be right about... there!*

He began to run, following the trail, feeling shells and gravel crunch underfoot. On his right, he saw the dock and slowed as he came to its foot. As he turned toward the lit-up house on the hill, a burst of heavy, masculine laughter carried from the house over the sound of the wind and rain. A door banged. Someone crossed the porch and started another car. The lights came on, the engine revved, and the auto drove away, lights sweeping across the rainy sky. There was another burst of laughs from the house and a woman's shrill scream, cut short.

At the scream, Dugan came up on his toes and dashed headlong up the gravel trail, caution forgotten and a cold chill in his heart that wasn't from the weather. The scream was a despairing, terrified scream, and someone had cut it off. He wasn't even conscious of the hill or the wind pushing him along. Coming toward the side of the house, he could see the lights in the back, the low porch, and the steps that led up to the front door.

Then he was on the porch, quietly through the door, and into the dim front room, all his senses focused on the doorway down the hall. He paused for a moment, chest heaving. He pulled the 9mm from his back pocket, drawing and snapping the safety off in one movement. Ahead, where the light spilled out around a half-opened door, he could hear male laughter, loud and cruel, with Spanish words roughly spoken and taunting. And sobs.

At least she's still alive, he thought. As he headed for the door, a floorboard creaked. There was sudden silence, a rough command, and the door pushed open to frame a man in the light.

Dugan was wet, tired, battered by the storm, and in a hurry. He didn't break stride as the doorway opened. The last thing the man in the doorway saw in the dim light was the outline of an oncoming man with three flashing explosions in his right hand as Dugan triple-tapped the 9mm. The little bullets ripped into the thug's chest.

As the dying Zeta went rigid in agony and began to fall back, Dugan pushed past him into the brightly lit room. He had the briefest impression of a blur of pink on a bed as he focused on the nearest man and tapped him too, this time in the forehead. Skull and cranial matter exploded against the wall.

In frozen time, Dugan sensed the last man standing was going for his gun in his discarded trousers on the other side of Riley's bed. In that split-second of time, Dugan felt his 9mm jam, and without a pause, threw it at the third man's head. Coming over the bed, Dugan smashed his elbow into the man's face, smacking his half-drawn pistol away. The man bounced off the wall and came back at Dugan like an uncaged tiger, all swinging arms, kicking legs, and biting teeth. For a moment, the sheer ferocity of the attack stopped the agent.

The day before, he'd have ended the fight before the Zeta even got close, but Dugan was worn down. The frantic attacker raked him across the face and tried to knee him before Dugan's head cleared. Dugan spun right and aimed for the back of the neck, but the clip went wide. The thug rolled to the side, kicking toward Dugan's knee. The agent dodged, then waded in with a chop at the man's Adam's apple and another slug across an ear.

Then the Zeta was back on him, and Dugan was in trouble. Dugan was bigger and probably more skilled, but he was also drained, and his opponent was rested and tough. Now they were jammed in the corner between the wall and the bed, and the crowded space made the thug's desperate energy count for more. He snarled, swung widely at Dugan's head. He connected with a clubbed punch that rattled Dugan down to his toes.

Dugan dropped into a fighter's crouch as the other man reached for his arm. Dugan slapped his hand away and crossed a right to his nose, hoping to see blood spurt. The Zeta only grunted and grappled Dugan's arm again, obviously intending a desperate throw. Dugan heaved to get away, but the thug twisted and gripped Dugan around the body, tried to lift him up.

Both men hurled to the floor, bouncing off the wall and the side of the bed on the way down, scrabbling like schoolyard wrestlers to get a grip on the other. As their bodies fought for purchase, the Zeta's fingers found Dugan's eyes. The agent twisted his head away while grabbing for the Zeta's throat, his eyes, then his ears—anywhere to get a grip.

This was desperate, no-holds fighting; each man knew that only one of them was going to walk away. They rolled two or three times on the rug and bumped the bed. Then the Zeta broke away and staggered to his feet. Dugan was up with him, and both men started swinging at the same moment. The man looped a wide left at Dugan. The agent stepped inside the wild punch and hammered his opponent in the face with a one-two, then stepped back and kicked the Zeta in the crotch with every ounce of energy he still had.

The man gasped, fell back on the bed, doubled over. Dugan grabbed the hair on the stunned man's head and smashed his head on Dugan's knee. He was doubled over and moaning when Dugan stooped over to lock his head under his arm; a lift, a sharp, hard twist, and the man's neck snapped with an audible pop. He jerked rigid, went limp, and flopped back on the bed and its occupant.

The fighting madness was on Dugan long enough to jerk the man up, throw the corpse on the floor, and give the man's head a solid kick to make sure the job was finished. Through the haze and bright points of red that comes with rage, Dugan knew not to leave a living enemy behind him, broken neck or not; some people live with broken necks. But the Zeta was done. Empty eyes stared up at the ceiling, and Dugan knew he wasn't going to make trouble anymore, not for him or anyone else.

The fight had been brutal and savage, and Dugan was beyond tired. He bent over and took a couple of whooshing breaths, scooped up somebody's black Beretta from the floor, automatically checked to be sure a round was in the chamber. He snapped on the safety and stuck the piece in his hip pocket. Then he looked at the bed.

Cassandra Riley was stripped nude and tied spread-eagled to the bed. Her tangled red hair was mostly over her face, but he could see her wild eyes and hear her panicked breathing. She was beyond crying and even whimpering, instead making little "whuff, whuff" sounds that someone makes just before they hyperventilate. There were bruises on her face and body.

In the instant he turned to her, he doubted she could have understood anything after she had been beaten and tied—not the gunshots, not the fight, not that she was safe now. *Relatively speaking*, Dugan thought.

He looked quickly around at the three corpses as he pulled the little knife from its sheath. One man was nude from the waist down, a detail Dugan had overlooked in the rush of things.

At least Cassandra Riley was alive, and after a little more head kicking to make sure that the rest of the crowd on the floor was truly dead, Dugan spoke to her gently as he cut the ropes holding her to the bed. He was in the process of pulling loose a sheet to cover her when she bolted like a big-eyed deer, panicked and lightning-fast toward the door. He dropped his knife and grabbed at her to keep her from running out into the storm, and instantly he was in another fight, this time with a panicked, nude woman stumbling blindly over dead men as she clawed her way into the hall.

Fear made her strong. Dugan chased her into the front room, covering her with the sheet as he got his arms around her to pull her down to the carpet. The arms she tried to use to hit and scratch his face were tangled up in the sheet, but she was driven with the steel-hard strength of last-ditch desperation. Dugan held onto her with his head tucked down, away from her fingernails, as he kept talking to her, soothing her, and telling her he was there to help, not hurt her.

Chapter 24

Wednesday 2100

After a second, she went limp and started to scream a quiet, desperate scream, an end-of-the-world scream. Dugan couldn't really blame her. Her pleasant life in Brewer was now a continuous, never-ending nightmare. Her daughter had been taken away, and she herself was a prisoner of men who she must have known were going to kill her. She had been beaten, stripped, and tied down. There was no hope.

And now here he was, so soaked and muddy from his run up the hill that she must have felt like the Swamp Thing was grabbing her. The two of them lay there on the carpet, Dugan gradually easing off his grip as her screams became sobs.

"You're okay now. It's going to be all right," Dugan repeated again and again. Even as he said them, he knew those lines probably made no sense to a woman who thought her world had ended. Dugan could just as well have recited the Gettysburg Address, but perhaps the tone penetrated. Maybe she simply ran out of energy. In the semidarkness, Dugan could see her push the hair out of her face, and she drew a ragged breath.

"Cassandra, it's okay now," he whispered. At the sound of her name, she stiffened.

"Who are you?" she demanded. "Why are you doing this to me?" Her voice was louder than it should be, as she was gathering strength.

"I know this is tough to take," Dugan said, keeping his voice low, "but I'm a friend. The best friend you've got right now."

"Where's my daughter?" She started to struggle again. "Let me go!"

"Cassandra, if I let you go, will you just sit quietly while I tell you what's going on?" He was watching the window behind her for lights in the driveway and listening for other movement in the house. The 9mm he picked up after the fight was still in his pocket, but with his arms occupied with Cassandra Riley, he couldn't draw it.

"If you keep making noise, somebody will try to kill us both," Dugan said, helpfully. She became very still, and the sobs stopped, though he could feel her chest rising and falling rapidly. The wind buffeted the house, and the sound partially covered their words. The rain beat harder on the windows. It was a grand nor'easter.

After a minute, her breathing became more regular. They both sat up on the carpet in the hall. Dugan released his grip, sitting back to give her space. She crossed her arms in front of her. In the dim light, Dugan grabbed the tangled sheet between them, pulled it loose, and handed it to her. She took it without comment and wrapped it around her like an oversized bath towel. The movement was so unconsciously genteel that Dugan knew she was coming back from whatever dark place she'd retreated to. He could just make out her face, hair straggling, eyes wide, an ugly bruise starting on her cheek. Only the truth would work now. So he told the truth again.

"I'm an agent of the U.S. government. I know what's going on. I know you've been held prisoner. I know your daughter has been kidnapped." He took a deep breath. "We've got to get the hell out of here."

She didn't start screaming again, which was a plus. There was a pause. "Well, it can't get any worse, can it?" she finally said. Her voice was shaky, but under control.

The lady has steel, Dugan thought.

"Who are you?" she asked.

His guess was she would not take lies well. "My name is Neil Dugan. I really am a legitimate government agent. Is there anybody else here in the house?"

"The big guy left. Felix, or whatever his name is, and one of the others. He went somewhere but told his... *men,*" she spit out the word, "that he was coming back." She swallowed and held her arms out, one at a time, as Dugan fumbled with the remains of the cheap cords that were still tied around her wrists. She let him work without interfering. She didn't give a damn anymore.

"He wouldn't let them... let them... Well, he told them to keep me until he came back." She gulped but maintained her composure. "I guess they decided not to wait. They've been watching me for days." She shuddered, then drew breath.

Dugan's anger rose again. She had been very, very close to death. Dugan was sure Guzmann would be coming back full of anticipation. But with Cassandra Riley on his hands, Dugan wasn't inclined to wait for him and his goons.

"Cassandra, can you walk? Did they... hurt you beyond the beating?"

"Did they rape me? No. The three of them pushed me into the bedroom and... stripped off my clothes. They hit me and then tied me down. They were laughing. Then the explosions, gunshots, fighting—I suppose that was you. But they didn't... they didn't..." She stopped.

He took her hand. She didn't move away, so he helped her to her feet. One hand held the sheet at her throat as she swayed for a moment and then sat down quickly in one of the overstuffed chairs.

Dugan knelt beside the chair, waited a second, and then said softly, "Cassandra, I need to check the house, and you need to get dressed. Then we need to get rid of the men in that room and get out of here. Can you help me?"

She nodded, pulling herself together with a visible effort. She shivered. The front door was still open from Dugan's entry, and the room was icy cold. He stepped over, closing the door to the storm.

"Stay here close to the door. If I'm not back in five minutes, or if you hear shooting, grab anything you can wear and run away from town. Can you do that?"

She nodded.

Actually, he'd given her lousy advice, but a risk of death by exposure would be better than what these people offered. Dugan squeezed her hand and soft-footed back down the hall and up the stairs, where he figured the electronics would be.

They were there all right, in the first guest suite at the head of the stairs, sharing space with a big four-poster bed. The place smelled like dirty socks. The lights were on and nobody was home. Dugan felt a wave of relief. He was in no shape for another prizefight.

He saw three black boxes and a swivel chair in the center of the room, where a single operator could watch them all. The boxes showed clusters of different instruments with LEDs lit up. They were going on with their work without benefit of human supervision.

On the biggest box, Dugan recognized the trademark of a mid-scale intrusion detection company; one of those outfits that promises the business owner peace of mind and scares the hell out of the employees when deer come into the parking lot and trip the alarm. The face of the box held three small, four-by-four, green-light screens that showed the woods and the driveway up to the Admiral's Arms.

So they used infrared after all, Dugan thought. The second box was apparently the direction-finding gadget that pinpointed Dugan's cell phone transmissions that morning. The instrument's face had words like "signal strength" and "azimuth" under blank windows that he supposed would show digital numbers if triggered.

The final one, the box nearest the door, had Cyrillic writing on it Dugan couldn't read, but an antenna lead ran out under the window. It had to be the connection to the gang's own low-power cell tower, probably to the antenna he had seen a few hours ago from his hiding position. Nearby was a cardboard box with a dozen or so cheap black flip phones, still in their convenience-store see-through packages, and a scattered bunch of charge cards.

Signal central, Dugan thought. *The weakness that brought their whole operation crashing down.*

He was in a hurry, so he didn't stop to figure everything out. He found the power strip, unplugging the motion detector and direction finder, but he decided to leave the cell tower working, since it could work for him, too. He spotted a cell phone lying on a desk and thrust it into his soaked jeans. Then he made a very quick visual inspection of the other three suites but found only unmade beds and dirty sheets.

He clattered back downstairs, down the hall to the cold, darkened living room. To his relief, Cassandra was still there, big-eyed in her sheet but more focused. She was no longer shaking. As he knelt again beside the chair, Dugan figured he'd been gone less than two minutes.

"Time to get dressed and get out of here," he said softly. "Are you up for it?"

She took a deep breath. "My clothes are in the room where they… where they stripped me," she said. "Will you come back with me?"

Dugan nodded.

Wordlessly, still wrapped in her sheet, she walked down the hall and into the bedroom, where the three bodies in various attitudes of death lay sprawled on the floor. There was the odor of urine. Looking straight ahead, she dropped the sheet and walked naked to a chest of drawers.

Dugan focused his eyes on the dead men but could hear her rummaging through her dresser. A second drawer opened. When he risked a glance back, Cassandra was automatically running her fingers through her tangled hair. She took only a moment to dress, pulling on underwear, a bulky sweater, and woolen socks.

Still looking straight ahead, she went to the closet and tugged on the door, but the half-nude body of one of Guzmann's finest blocked it. Wide-eyed and with just a touch of panic, she tugged again. Dugan grabbed the corpse under the arms and pulled it away.

She whispered, "Thank you," and giggled, just on the edge of hysteria. Then she mastered herself. She pulled out a pair of hiking boots, walking unsteadily back to the front room to pull them on and to tie the laces. She picked up a waterproof jacket lying on a couch. As she turned to Dugan, he could see the tears as she fought for sanity. She was a tough lady, but the scene in the bedroom was almost too much.

"Come out on the porch with me," he said. He led her out of the house on the side away from the wind, to a wicker settee that in normal times would have been brought inside before the storm. It was cold but bearable. If the weather bothered her, she gave no sign of it.

"We need to get my daughter," she said over the sound of the wind.

"We need to get away from here first," Dugan said, also pitching his voice to be heard over the roar of the nor'easter. "I've got a safe place. And then we'll get Erin. Stay here for a minute." He squeezed her hand and started to pull away, but she grabbed his hand in an iron grip and he stopped.

"How do you know about Erin?" she asked.

Dugan dropped to a knee beside the settee, facing past her to the house and the driveway.

"Cassandra, I know about Erin the same way I know about you. I know the story about these bastards who moved in on you. I know Erin has been taken away, and I know where she is." He squeezed her hand and said it again for emphasis. "I know where she is. And I know we're going to get her back, and everything is going to be okay. Okay?"

She took a long, shuddering breath. Even in the rain and wind, Dugan could sense her steeling herself.

"Listen, mister, I don't care about you or whatever game you're up to. I don't give a damn. Unless you can tell me, *right now,* how this works to get Erin back, you can go to hell."

Chapter 25

She drew a deep breath. "I appreciate what you've done for me. God, I really do." Her voice thickened up and started to rise, and then she again climbed down from the edge of hysteria with a shudder. "But Erin... if you can't... if you can't take me to her, I'm going myself."

Over her shoulder, Dugan could see the light in the bedroom. He was sure Guzmann would be back and dealing with him now would raise complications. Dugan was on a timetable, and a lot still had to be done. He didn't need a hysterical mother on his hands, but her priorities were right. She wasn't going to help unless she knew what was going on and trusted him.

"Cassandra," Dugan said, projecting all the quiet urgency he could. "This is how it works. A lot of people, me included, are going to risk our lives tonight to get Erin back. And the others from the town. We're pretty good at what we do. But I need your help now, and if you help me, we both help Erin. Otherwise, you'll just run into more people like those three back there, and Erin's no better off." *Actually,* he thought, *she's a lot worse off, and so is her mom.*

There was silence. In the dim light Dugan could see her shivering again, either from the cold or from her very close brush with death. Her tangled hair hung over her tear-streaked face, and her eyes found his. Then she brushed her hair back, and he heard her intake of breath and saw the brief attempt at a smile.

"Okay. I've got it. Let's do what we have to do and get the hell out of here, like you said." Her hand found Dugan's, and she gave it a quick squeeze.

After everything, he thought the squeeze was a hopeful sign, and he squeezed back. It felt good. But now there was work to do. He pulled her inside the house again and back to the settee.

"Wait here," he said. "If you see car headlights, come and get me." He went back to the ruined bedroom with the cut cords on the four-poster bed and the three bodies on the floor. First, he picked up his little knife from where he'd dropped it and slipped it back into its sheath. Then he checked again to be sure the men were certainly dead.

They were. Their bodies sprawled out as only dead men can, and their glazing eyes stared sightlessly at the walls and ceiling. In their pockets, Dugan found some loose change, a matchbox from some place in Baltimore, and two more phones Dugan crammed in his pockets. Next, he looked around for their guns and found two more of the black military-grade Berettas where each man dropped or threw them during the fight.

They must be buying these things by the case, he thought.

Both guns were loaded, and the magazines were full. Dugan walked into the living room and dropped the two pistols onto the sofa. Back in the bedroom, he grabbed the nearest body under the arms, dragged the corpse onto a braided throw rug, and dumped it there. He reversed ends and took hold of the body by the ankles, using the rug to slide down the hall, through the living room, past Cassandra to the front door, carefully sticking to the wood floor between the lush area rugs.

When he got to the door, he gave the ankles a hard yank, dragging the body across the wood porch and down the stairs in one sustained movement. The man's head bounced on each step. At the bottom, the wind blew so hard, the rain streaked almost horizontally.

Dugan walked wearily back up the steps and into the living room where Cassandra waited. As he walked past her, he noticed her hair was somehow settled down, and she looked like she was returning to the world. She shivered, but now it was cold, not panic. He ducked into the bedroom, came out with the two 9mms, and handed her one.

"You know how to use this thing? he asked.

She hefted the pistol, feeling the grip. "I do. Is there a round in the chamber?"

Dugan wondered how much she really knew. "Why don't you chamber one and find out?"

She gripped the slide like a pro, yanked it back, and released it. The 9mm round in the chamber ejected and landed at his feet, and he heard the *snick* of another one going into the chamber.

She looked defiantly up at Dugan. "Satisfied?" she asked.

"I am. Put the safety on and keep watching for headlights. If you see lights, run like hell to me, and we'll get out of here." He went back to the corpse at the bottom of the stairs.

From there it was a relatively easy pull down to the dock. In the darkness and rain, it was fairly simple to pull the body onto the dock and roll it off into the water beside the pier. Dugan figured the four feet deep water was enough to hide the corpses from any kind of a hasty search. Then he went back for the others.

Dead bodies are heavy, limp, and notoriously hard to handle. Dugan was exhausted by the time the other two corpses had been rolled into the dark water alongside the first.

While Dugan dragged the bodies to the water, Cassandra had stopped shaking. He took it as a hopeful sign that she was more worried about the next few minutes than memories of the scene in her bedroom.

There was still a picture to paint in the bedroom. It didn't take long, but by the time Dugan finished, Guzmann and his *compadres* would see the cut cords, the rumpled bed, and the blood and assume the three missing lads got carried away, and the body of the gringo lady was being dumped somewhere.

At least the evidence they could see pointed that way, and in their hurry, they might be satisfied with easy answers, or at least wouldn't have time to look elsewhere. Meanwhile, weariness washed through his body. *Getting too old for this,* he thought. He sat down beside Cassandra in the dark living room with his head between his legs and took a few deep breaths. Cassandra gripped her pistol, watched for headlights, and sensibly remained silent as Dugan reached back for his reserves of energy. After some moments, his wind came back, and without speaking, he stood and held out his hand. It was time to leave.

Wordlessly, she put her hand in his, and the two headed for the bay. As they came around the corner of the house, the wind and rain hit them with a physical force, pushing them back until they had to bend forward and force their way downhill into the storm. When they got to the base of the hill, they turned right at the pier. Dugan led her along the water's edge and into the brush and weeds when the path became indistinct and overgrown. Going back toward town was faster than Dugan's cautious approach only an hour before. With the deadline approaching and Guzmann's shrinking workforce, Dugan decided surveillance was unlikely along the water's edge. In the upstairs room, there had been no indications of sensors deployed toward the town or waterfront. He walked ahead at a fast pace, holding Cassandra's hand, almost pulling her along and bulling his way through the grasses and scrub oaks until they got to the outskirts of Brewer.

Dugan slowed their pace as they wove among the buildings. Half-running and stumbling, but with Cassandra's hand still in his, Dugan came up behind the old crab packing shed from the west side, with a line of retreat behind them in case they decided to run. The town, with all its shadows and closed spaces, could be a deathtrap if Guzmann and his boys came in shooting. Dugan was fairly optimistic that Jonah and the trussed-up thugs were still secure.

With memories of two 12-gauge pumps in his mind, Dugan threw pebbles against one of the windows until he sensed a face in the darkness, then whispered Jonah's name. There was silence, and then the weather-beaten door opened without a sound or without any sign of anybody. Dugan stayed put, Cassandra crouching beside him.

"Hey, First Team," he whispered urgently, using the First Cavalry Division's nickname. "It's the good guys. Don't shoot."

There was a chuckle from the darkness inside and Jonah's low rumble. "Man, yo' better come in outa the rain and bring the lady with you."

Dugan and Cassandra eased into the greater darkness inside the building. The noise of the storm was cut off abruptly as the door closed behind them. They were in a gloomy world barely lit by the dim, blue glow of the space heater. The warmth of the room hit them like a blow. Dugan was shivering. A glance showed that Cassandra was shaking too, and he moved to give her room around the heater.

"Anything from Deion?" But he was wasting his breath. Cassandra and Jonah were having a reunion, hugging each other like Dugan didn't exist.

"Cassy, we didn't know they got you too."

"Are your mother and father—"

"Off with everybody else," he said. "And Deion's folks, Mitzie, and the baby."

"Oh, Jonah, I'm so sorry," she said. "They took Erin and moved into the Arms. I've been cooking and housekeeping for those sons of bitches since then." There would never be a time to mention the scene in the bedroom.

"We're going to get them back," Dugan said. Jonah and Cassandra turned to him and waited silently. "Counting Deion, there are four of us, and we've got guns, and ah, some help coming." More silence. He began to explain.

Chapter 26

We have to get moving, Dugan thought when he paused for breath. He raised his arm, pushing the little illumination button on his watch again to check the time. Close.

"Jonah, what's the word on our guests?" he asked. They were a complication and keeping them out of play was important.

"They're okay. Still tied up like pigs in a poke. The blond guy asked if I could loosen his ropes." He laughed quietly. "No kidding. He really said that."

"We have to move." Dugan turned to Cassandra. In the dim light of the kerosene heater, he could just make out the shape of her face and the shine of her eyes.

"Cassandra, I've got a tough job for you." Dugan looked around for the other shotgun, and Jonah put it into his hand.

"It's loaded all the way up," the big man said.

Dugan jacked the slide, felt a shell go into the chamber, and snapped the safety on. Even in the darkness, he could sense Cassandra's intensity.

"Here's a twelve-gauge," he said, putting the gun into her hands, then indicating the men tied up on the floor. "These two bozos are going to wind up under the hot lights." He paused. Leaving her alone was going to be tough for a lady who was on the

145

verge of being raped and killed just an hour or so before. On the other hand, it might just give her the edge she needed.

"They are part of cleaning up this mess. If they get loose, they can screw the whole deal. If they're still alive when this is over, they will probably have something to say. But it's keeping them from screwing the deal that is most important. Keeping them alive is really only incidental."

Dugan found her hand and put her fingers on the safety in the dark, then pushed it back and forth, feeling the click. "Here's the safety."

She nodded in the dimness and pulled her hand away. "I hunt. I know shotguns."

"Great." For some reason, the way her fingers felt lingered briefly in his mind. "Listen to what I say very, very carefully. If either of these two begins to move in a threatening way or yell, I want you to kill them both. Just point the gun and pull the trigger. Pump and pull the trigger again."

"God."

"No, God comes later, I guess," Dugan said. "But if these guys get loose, they can kill you, Erin, and a bunch of other people."

"God."

"Come to think of it, if they move at all, shoot them. These men are pros. Shoot on any suspicion."

She nodded again, took the gun, and pointed it at the floor.

Dugan was liking Cassandra Riley more and more. He walked over to the trussed-up figures lying on the cement floor, then gently nudged the Hispanic in the head with his boot. The man grunted but made no other noise.

"*Senor,*" Dugan said in conversational Spanish. "You will listen to what I say." He took a step and nudged the blond as well. "Do you both hear me?" There was no sound, so he kicked the first man little harder. "*Mi amigo,*" he said. "I can kick even harder. It is a little thing to listen."

146

The figure on the floor grunted and nodded, just as Dugan was poised for another kick.

"My friends and I are going outside for a while, but we will be near. The *senora* will be here with you." He gave the second man a dig with his toe too, just to encourage him to listen.

"She will be alone and knows you are bad people," Dugan continued in Spanish. "She has a 12-gauge shotgun. I have told her if either of you moves, she is to kill you both with the shotgun and shoot until she has no ammunition left. Do you hear me?"

The conversationalist grunted around his gag. It might have been *si*. The blond remained silent.

Spanish may not have been his language after all. But they've been warned, Dugan thought.

"She has a daughter you took away from her. I have told her if you were to escape, her daughter will be in danger. I think she will kill you both with pleasure."

Dugan turned back to Cassandra. She seemed to smile in the darkness. "It would be a great pleasure," she said in perfect Spanish, just loud enough for them to hear. "I will kill you if you move in the slightest. And I will shoot first in your manhood and perhaps let you linger that way."

She turned to look at Dugan in the dim light. "I've been speaking Spanish since I was a girl," she said in English. "Those bastards at the house didn't know. I listened to everything they said."

She kicked the Hispanic in the side. "My daughter and I have suffered because of trash like you," she said, again in impeccable Spanish. "Please give me a reason to kill you."

Hallelujah, Dugan thought. He left her with the shotgun and the captives. He walked into the other room and put the kerosene heater beside the door, where Cassandra could see the captives by its light and have warmth. He swung an old battered folding chair to the door should she feel inclined to sit. He dug in his soaked jeans pocket and pulled out his keys. He held them out to her.

"Here are my car keys," Dugan said. "It's the gray Ford in front of the garage. Just in case. I want you to sit here watching these two until Deion gets back. Then the two of you just sit tight, and when the cops come, one of you go out and get somebody. The cops will take it from there."

By the time Deion got back, Dugan figured the other side would have pulled back into the Walker house to be ready for the final act. He didn't think it was necessary to spell out that the first good guys they were going to see weren't going to be cops exactly. Simplicity was the name of the game here.

"Erin?" The lady was focused on the two on the floor, but her voice had a plea.

"By then Erin will be released, and you'll see her soon. I will bring her to you myself." *Another tradecraft violation—getting personally involved. Sal was going to have a full-blown cat.* he thought. *Screw Sal.*

"But if everything goes to hell—and I don't think it will—but if you get scared or think too much time has gone by or anything doesn't feel right—anything at all—shoot these guys, run to my car, and drive out of here. Just go and go fast. And once you're miles out of town, call this number." Dugan scribbled something on a piece of the paper Jonah had given him.

"Tell whoever answers that you have a message for Sal from Neil." He added the two names with the phone number, a gross violation of security, but Sal would instantly recognize that whoever sent a message from Neil had to be genuine.

"Keep insisting until you talk to him. Then you'll have lots of company—of the right kind." Dugan gave her the paper.

She started to say something, but he interrupted her. "You aren't really going to need the car," he said. "There's going to be some shooting at the old Walker place, and then Erin and you will be safe. But remember, if there is any question of you being threatened at all, or if you are the least bit uneasy and want to take the car and get away, shoot these two here first. Do not hesitate. Kill them."

She nodded, hefted the gun, snapped the safety a few times, then wordlessly sat down in the old folding chair against the wall. The two figures on the floor were perfectly still.

Maybe they understand what I just told her, Dugan thought. *They certainly heard the part about their manhood.* He gave her shoulder a squeeze, and she briefly touched his hand with hers, but she never took her eyes off the two tied-up forms.

Chapter 27

A minute later, Jonah and Dugan eased out the back of the shed into the storm and headed for the woods on the east side. The nor'easter still blew in full force. The rain stung their cheeks like hard pellets, and the wind came in gusts that topped forty knots. Dugan moved with one hand protecting his eyes. Jonah bowed his head to the storm, his face mostly protected by the bill of his cap.

Dugan led the way with the 9mm handgun taken from the inn, while Jonah carried his 12-gauge like the trained soldier he was—high up and slantwise across his chest, ready to cut down or butt stroke up. *Whoever trained him found a natural,* Dugan thought. He glanced at his watch. After nine. Almost enough time had gone by for a ship to pass from the Chesapeake Bridge to the Potomac. *There might be enough time for Sal's plan to work if Deion gets through, or if Sal or someone just decides to trigger it and take a chance on the hostages.*

Through the trees on the right a quarter mile away, Dugan could see the lights of the old Walker place. If the lights were any indication, the thugs had no idea anything was about to happen—the place was ablaze. He put his mouth to Jonah's ear.

"You know the ground. I figure to come in off the side of the road. They'll have outposts, but they probably won't be very good in this weather."

He paused to gather his thoughts, then went on. "I don't think we need to worry about sensors. I disabled most of them up at the inn, and even if they have remotes from the systems, the weather is so crappy, they probably won't believe them. But they might have guards. Let me lead when we get close."

Jonah nodded, took the lead, and navigated them through the wet brush. They moved together in the dark, Dugan watching their rear.

After a hundred yards, they came to the dirt road that ran out to the peninsula and the Walker place. Without a word, Jonah changed course and the men paralleled the road, keeping ten to fifteen yards inside the woods and lower brush. It was slow going. Even in the storm, they were alert for sentries so each of them walked carefully, easing a foot down, rocking forward as the weight shifted from one leg to another, and then another slow step.

Fifteen minutes later, when Dugan guessed they were within a hundred meters, he stretched out his arm and laid a hand on Jonah's shoulder. The big veteran nodded, eased down to one knee as Dugan slow walked past him for ten meters, then also went down on a knee.

Now was the hard part. Dugan took a quick look at the dim illumination of his watch and figured they had to wait half an hour, maybe less. He settled in, relaxing his muscles slightly and resting back on his knee, still high enough to see but not so high that a sweep with night vision glasses would pick him out against the background. Or so he hoped. Even in the storm, he was comfortable in the woods at night. He had learned to sit quietly in the night for hours, lessons reinforced by hunting and his later, more specialized training. He drifted off into a sort of semi-consciousness, with one part of his brain alert, hearing and sensing everything, closed to the discomfort of the soaking rain and the cold. He was conscious of being bone-tired without any suggestion of sleep. Once or twice something moved, and he went to full alert, then relapsed into waiting. Jonah had to shift now and then, though he never made a noise.

Despite the miserable weather, the time passed quickly for the two men kneeling in the bushes. The wind slacked, and it started to rain harder again. Dugan felt the rain on his skin, his face, and his hands, which shook from the cold. But the cold rain never penetrated to his inner core, and he sensed Jonah felt the same inner heat. The hunt was on, and both men ignored the weather, focused on bigger game.

After a long wait, Dugan checked his watch again. Time to go. He raised his hand to catch Jonah's attention and then slowly moved awkwardly off his stiff leg and felt the tingle as the blood started to flow again. With Jonah behind him, he eased forward a dozen yards then stopped for a long minute, listening, and trying to guess where the guards would be, if they were out at all. The wind and rain would go a long way toward neutralizing them but getting discovered prematurely would risk the whole mission.

Most of the lights in the house were now turned off, except for a few dim leaks from behind shutters and blinds that showed the house was still occupied. The light-leaks were useful guides as he and Jonah emerged from the woods and into a scrubby area that had once been a field. They approached the house until they were fifty yards from a line of tall pines planted between the house and the field as a windbreak. As they moved, a single light in the window of the boathouse and a few more lights came on inside the main house. They passed the old mansion, headed toward the boathouse, and heard the loud guttural voices from the house.

Dugan froze and concentrated on hearing. Even with the rain, sounds were magnified in the darkness, and he strained to hear footsteps, cars starting, or in the worst case, alarms, followed by the remaining gunmen piling out of the house with submachine guns against a 9mm pistol and a 12-gauge. But no alarms came. Dugan was certain the light was on in the boathouse to prepare the go-fast for its final mission, and that the other pieces of his and Sal's operation were coming together.

With less caution, he rose to his feet and rushed toward a line of black and indistinct hedge pines between him and the house. Behind him, he heard Jonah get to his feet and follow, his footfalls oddly muted for a large man. Together, they reached the pines without being shot, hit the soggy ground side by side, and lay with their heads together twenty yards from the house. Jonah was puffing a little, but to Dugan, he seemed to be in pretty good shape for a middle-aged guy who'd been pumping gas and adding a little to his belly each year.

Dugan whispered, "The show is about to start." A sixth sense told him, that out there in the wind and the rain, there were blacker shapes on the water, and time was running out. "I think there's about to be a lot of shooting, and we need to get inside that house. That's where your people are, and that's where we need to be."

"Let's do it," Jonah said.

Dugan felt him tense for the sprint across the open ground.

Dugan spotted another familiar black SUV between the fringe of trees and the house. "The car," he whispered, jumped to his feet, and took off for it at a dead run, zigzagging through the dark rain and hoping attention was diverted elsewhere. He slammed to a stop next to the forward wheel and a second later Jonah dropped beside him. The rear door to the house was fifty feet away.

Dugan turned and again put his mouth next to Jonah's ear. "We won't get away free next time. Watch the window. Shoot anybody with a gun."

He focused on the door, got to his feet, and ran toward the house. The big shotgun suddenly boomed behind him, briefly illuminating the side of the house, and ending in a scream and the crash of broken glass. Dugan's shoulder slammed into the door, and he crashed into a kitchen. The room was filled with the dark shapes of boxes, crates, and old cans, and a dank, musty smell. All this crowded in on his senses as the world outside erupted in gunfire and chaos, with the rattle of automatic-weapons fire and the flash-bang of stun grenades. Jonah crashed through the door, pushed Dugan aside, and charged into the house. Dugan ran behind, and it was like following a charging bull.

Room-to-room fighting is dry-mouth, short-range, spine-tingling fear. Most men, even when well trained, only fight that way unwillingly and cautiously. Not Jonah. He roared and swore as he rampaged down the corridors of the old Walker place. Without pausing in his charge down the halls, he blew a 12-gauge hole in a man with a pistol who took a shot and missed. He kicked doors open and rushed in muzzle-first. His shotgun blasted a second man into a bloody heap. But even in his blind rage, Jonah's finger on the trigger was steady. Dugan ran behind him, an awed accessory to Jonah's storm.

After the first three doors, they found them—people cowering in corners, kids crowded together, old people tied to beds, and the smell of unwashed bodies and toilets everywhere. Grim-faced old men. Big-eyed women. Just impressions in the dimness as the two men looked for the monsters who had captured these innocents.

A word, a hand wave, and Dugan followed Jonah down the corridors of the second floor, where the doors to the big rooms opened out. A shotgun blast again and screams. Jonah jumped over a bloody body, his arms out toward two older people in the middle of the room.

"Ma! Pa!" he shouted. And suddenly Jonah's charge was over. The two were folded in his arms.

Outside, the chatter of automatic-weapons fire was more sporadic now. Dugan took a deep breath as bright lights started appearing outside. He leaned against a wall next to a shattered window.

"Friend!" he yelled through the broken glass. "Friend!"

"Behind you!" Jonah shouted.

Dugan made a diving turn, and a bullet clipped the windowsill, the muzzle flash from deeper in the house.

"Damn it!" he shouted as he fell. *Amateur mistake.* But before Dugan could get his own gun up, there was a thunking sound, like an axe hitting a stump, and the sound of a body falling.

"God*damn*," said a voice. "That was almost worth it."

Dugan rolled over and stared at the old man from the night before. A piece of wood resting on his shoulder, he was standing over the unconscious body of a blond European. Dugan got shakily to his feet.

The old man grinned and punched his shoulder. "Saw you last night. Tol' these folks there was a change coming. I marked this bastard," he said, kicking him hard in the side of the head. "Shithead sonofabitch."

Dugan realized he could see, so at least some of the inside lights had stayed on.

"Jonah, get these people all together in this room. Count noses. But nobody leaves until you hear different."

"Got it," Jonah said and began to gather the people, his big voice bellowing.

Dugan moved down the hall through the increasing crowd headed the other way. There was a towheaded little girl, all big eyes and tears.

"Erin?" he asked.

She nodded, mute. So much had happened.

He stopped and knelt. "I just came from your mommy. She's safe, and she loves you. She'll be here soon."

Erin nodded uncertainly. *God knows what I look like to a little girl,* he thought, *all muddy, wet, and scary.* There would be some trauma for a while, he realized. But it could have been far worse.

"Go with these people now. Do you know Jonah Miller? Runs the gas station?"

She nodded.

"Jonah and I are working with your mom. Go to him and stay there, and I'll take you to your mommy." Then, to Dugan's immense surprise, she gave him a wordless hug.

How often have I been hugged by a six-year-old? he thought and was surprised at how rewarded it made him feel.

Still without speaking, she disentangled herself and moved on down the hall with the crowd. Dugan took a deep breath, pushed against the crowd, elbowed his way past all the questions, and came out the back door.

.... And walked right into the muzzle of a submachine gun, held by a pair of remarkably steady hands. The black-faced character above the muzzle didn't look entirely sympathetic either, his eyes hard in a blackened face. Dugan stopped and was very still.

"I'm a friend," Dugan said. "Dogfight Six."

The eyes behind the machine gun did not move, but he did speak into a voice mike, barely moving his lips. Dugan remained absolutely still, and so did he.

After a moment, another black figure came up from behind. "Dogfight Six?"

"That's me," Dugan said. "Agent Smith."

"Roger, sir," the figure said in that clipped style familiar from so long ago. "Lieutenant Chin. Is the house secure?" The man holding the gun on Dugan relaxed.

"It is," Dugan said. "Enter with caution. Large African-American friend with a shotgun in charge. Name's Jonah Miller. About a hundred-plus people who will require food, medication, and accounting." *The interrogators are going to be busy for weeks,* he thought, *but these folks aren't going anywhere but home for now.*

A burst of gunfire erupted in the night, and everyone dropped to the ground. Dugan hoped Jonah would keep the townspeople away from the windows.

"Shit," Chin said. "They're still in the boathouse."

"They?" Dugan asked.

"Five or six were in the boathouse when we came ashore," Chin said. "We didn't know they were there until we were already rolling them up." There was another burst. "No time for a proper recon."

Dugan and Chin got to their feet and started toward the boathouse, crouched over. The third man stayed by the house.

Chin's SEALs formed a rough semicircle about fifty meters from the boathouse, just far enough out for squirt-gun automatic weapons fire to be less dangerous, but close enough to keep anyone in the boathouse from getting out. The people in the boathouse were finished, Dugan knew. Chin's people were bringing up breaching charges and anti-tank rockets. The patrol boat that delivered them would cut off seaward escape, and the other SEALs in waiting patrol craft would board the mother ship and take down the crew. Sal's plan was coming together.

Dugan, Chin, and his men were halfway across the space between the house and the water when they heard the roar of a very overstressed car engine. A bright beam of light swept across the dimly-lit scene, and Dugan's old motor-pool Ford charged into the middle of everything, throwing mud and skidding to a rocking, sliding stop in the middle of the no-mans' land between the gang in the boathouse and the black-suited SEALs spread behind the trees and outhouses around the water's edge.

"What the hell is *this?*" snarled Chin. He filled his lungs to begin shouting orders

Dugan took charge before Chin could, grabbing the SEAL commander's arm in his urgency, pitching his voice in the old way.

"Hold your fire! Hold your goddam fire!"

The superbly disciplined SEALS obeyed the authority in his voice.

There was a sudden silence after the mayhem a few seconds before. The passenger's side door slammed open. Cassandra tumbled out and hit the ground face first, her arms bound behind her. Bile rose in Dugan's throat.

Right behind her, Guzmann erupted from the backseat, grabbing Cassandra by the hair, and raising her face to the lights. His face was twisted with rage as he held the 12-gauge one-handed against her head, the muzzle next to her eye. He jerked her head further up by her hair and squinted into the headlights. A little blood trickled from Cassandra's lower lip. She opened her eyes, and something in Dugan screwed up tight.

"Hey, bastards," Guzmann yelled in a high falsetto. He pronounced it with a funny accent, *bee-stards.* "You see the lady, yes?" He jerked her hair again. She grimaced but made no noise. "You want I spread her brains around?" He jerked again, a sadist enjoying the pain he inflicted. A Latino guy Dugan hadn't seen before eased himself out of the driver's seat, a pistol in his hand and big, spaced-out eyes in the light.

Dugan said, "Chin, I want no funny tricks. Let this play out." The last thing he needed was some gung-ho boatswain's mate to try to take either one of these guys down. Guzmann held the shotgun crammed against Cassandra's face. She was one nervous twitch from death.

Chin spoke quietly and urgently into his throat mike, and the special operations troops were immobile.

"Ah," Guzmann said, "so she lives." He stood over her, the shotgun still beside her head. She looked like hell, struggling to stand with her arms pinioned behind her. Guzmann and the other Latino began backing toward the boathouse with Cassandra in front of them as a human shield. His shotgun never left her ear.

"Sir," Chin's voice was urgent. "What do you want from us?"

Dugan took a breath. "Hold what we have. Play his game until we understand it."

Guzmann and Cassandra stumbled backward up the steps to the door of the boathouse, the driver opened it, and they disappeared inside. The knot in Dugan's gut got tighter. The rain, now mixed with sleet, fell harder, and the pines moaned in the wind. There was a heartbeat of silence while the boathouse sat in the bright lights of the SEAL torches, then a sudden roar. In a split-second, the planks in the back of the boathouse disintegrated as the powerful boat surged out of the dock with engines on full throttle and headed out into the bay, wake and bow wave showing white against the black water, automatic-weapons fire winking from the stern.

With the boat bucking and pitching, they might as well have been shooting at the clouds, but for a split-second, the fire delayed whatever reaction the SEALs might have had. The boat disappeared into the curtain of rain and darkness.

Chapter 28

Not all the modifications on the Handy were done in the shipyards. Years of meticulous planning now would pay off, for on a mission so important to the Umma, no detail was overlooked. In the Atlantic and away from shoreside gossip, her rendezvous with the support ship brought not only the two nuclear devices, but also the other weapons that full preparation for the mission required. The weapons and the fire-control systems had been mounted around the ship by experts, against a remote possibility they would be needed.

The firefight on shore was apparent to the ship's crew through their infrared, even though the distance and the storm muted the sounds. Moments before, the weapons station operators identified a number of hostile targets surrounding the ship, gathered invisibly in the storm.

For the Handy's leader, it was the first real indication of trouble. He smiled as he stroked his beard, then gave instructions to the sheikh who controlled the ship's armament. In seconds, the electronic brains of ten MM40 Block Two Exocet missiles were awakened and shown their targets. The missiles left their launchers, dropped to two meters from the sea, and hunted down their prey.

"Hold your fire," Dugan yelled as he took off for the boathouse, afraid of what he would find. Chin was a step behind. Together, careless of any stay-behind covering force, they crashed through the door. Chin swept the place with a powerful torch he carried on his gear. But there was nothing, and no body, just pilings and the cut lines where the boat had been secured. Through the shattered door, the white water of the wake grew steadily more distant.

Dugan grabbed Chin's equipment harness. "Where are the SEAL boats? What did you bring?" he demanded.

Chin didn't seem to mind being grabbed. "Waiting offshore. A couple of SEAL delivery boats we launched from and two more Navy patrol boats loaded with SEALs to board the merchie. But they're not expecting—"

Out in the rain, there was a sudden glow, then another, then the sound of rippling explosions, then nothing. A moment later, a fireball briefly illuminated the tossing waves of the bay, and then it vanished.

An overwhelming weariness came over Dugan. He ran back toward the house, yelling orders at Chin. "Take charge of the people here. Get ahold of our control and tell him what's happened. Tell him I'm in hot pursuit."

Chin tried to speak but Dugan cut him off, the mad dog rising in him like a red fire. "Give me a big light or something I can use to see with."

"Jonah," Dugan shouted into the house. People were staggering out; everybody talking, crying, and hugging. A few SEALs with weapons slung were carrying kids. He briefly saw Deion hugging a woman. No time for his story.

"Jonah," Dugan yelled again. A big black shape came out of the crowd.

"Neil!" Jonah shouted back through the crowd. Dugan saw he still held the shotgun.

161

"The bastards have Cassandra!" Dugan yelled. "I need somebody who knows boats. You up for it?"

Jonah didn't even pause. "Bet your ass."

Dugan ran to the old green Ford. The keys were still in the ignition as he'd hoped. He was twisting the key when Chin ran up.

"Sir, here!" He tossed Dugan his black flashlight. "Good hunting!"

He was left behind as Dugan and Jonah roared away, bouncing back down the road toward town. Dugan vaguely remembered seeing the white workboat at the pier.

"Jonah, how do we start that boat at the end of the pier?"

"Man, you jes' ask me. That's my boat. I been using that boat for crabbin' and fishin' since I got back from the war."

They skidded to a stop near the shed looming in the wind and rain. The two men ran onto the slippery pier where the boat bobbed up and down. Dugan recognized the type, a common bay workboat of about twenty-five feet, built on the Boston Whaler model. Square bow, built-in flotation, flat hull, stand-up central wheel console with a windscreen, and a big outboard. Water sloshed in the bottom as the boat tugged at its bow and stern lines.

"They're headed for a ship where the river and the bay come together. Think you can navigate to there?" Dugan asked.

Without pausing Jonah jumped, sure-footed, into the surging boat and laughed, his voice booming against the wind. "Shee-it, man. Been crabbing' these waters all my life. Folks named me Jonah because it was a boat-soundin' name. This little storm don't matter. Good boat, we can handle whatever the bay got." He laughed, a high-pitched, maniacal sound as Dugan jumped less expertly from the pier into the wildly bobbing boat, crashing to his knees without feeling.

There was a madness between them. They both were on a high from the violence. They were frenzy-men, hunters, killers this night, out to kill more. Dugan had a flash of insight. *Some men live all their lives and never have this kind of exaltation. Sal was right. Berserking. My Black Dog.*

As Dugan worked his way toward the center console he yelled, "I thought you said you could start this thing?"

Jonah laughed again, produced a big pocketknife, and began to pry the back panel off the control console.

"Bastards took my keys," he said. "Just wanted the boat there for looks. But I started this boat before with no keys, sometimes when I just forget, you know?" There was a faint pinging sound, and Jonah grunted in satisfaction.

"Gimme some light, man!"

As the boat heaved and plunged at her moorings, Dugan braced himself against the center console and shined the big torch in the cavity behind the instrument panel. Even with the boat's surging motion, Jonah unhesitatingly put his big hand inside the console, felt around, and yanked out two wires. He let them hang in the storm while he briefly hauled himself to the operator's side of the console against the surging waves, pushed the throttle forward, and pulled out the choke. Then he switched back, grabbed the two exposed wires and peeled off old electrical tape, exposing bare copper.

He grinned at Dugan as he touched the two wires together. There was a spark, a momentary cough from the stern, and the big outboard on the transom of the boat began to rumble.

"Great motor, man," Jonah said. "Keep it tiptop. Now let's get after those sonsobitches."

Dugan dropped the big light in an equipment bin on the console, and he and Jonah separately moved to the taut bow and stern lines. Jonah released the stern and moved back to the helm while Dugan was fractionally slower with the bow cleat. The bow clipped the pilings as Jonah, behind the wheel at the stand-up central console, gunned the engine, and took the boat into the oncoming waves. Dugan staggered from the impact with the pilings, then fought to keep his footing as the square-bowed workboat began to shoulder through the oncoming seas.

They headed directly into the storm, throwing freezing spray on both sides as they pulled away from the land. Dugan mentally pulled up the chart of the bay, determined the direction to the junction of the Potomac with the bay, and waved his arm to Jonah, nearly invisible behind the windscreen.

The big man nodded and shoved the throttles forward. With a roar, the little boat charged ahead. In less than a minute, it was clear of the inlet and into the open bay, where big waves began to throw the workboat from side to side. In response, Jonah rammed the throttles all the way forward, and the boat accelerated and planed, now hammering from wave to wave instead of randomly pitching and tossing as before. It was an improvement, but not much.

In the maelstrom of darkness, flying spray, and the roar of the engines, Dugan found a handhold on the console, looped his arm around it, and shouted over the sound of the engine and the crashing waves. "We need to guess where the mother ship will be. I think somewhere around the mouth of the river."

He knew Jonah was an experienced waterman, but the junction of the Potomac and the bay was a huge body of water, rough on the best days. The storm severely cut back visibility, not to mention that they were out on the water in survival conditions. If they didn't get some help, even Jonah would be steering blind.

If Jonah was discouraged, he didn't look it. He nodded at Dugan, squinted at the invisible compass on the console, gave it up, and looked ahead. Dugan did too, but it didn't do much good. They and the boat were in a black and dark tunnel. Black for the water over the side, a slightly lighter shade for the horizon. The rain fell hard enough to hold down the whitecaps, leaving surging waves that didn't break.

There were no lights ahead. The bay chop was three or four feet, which was a punishing speed for a flat-bottomed boat, and

Dugan wondered briefly if the outboard motor mount could handle it for long. Although the console windscreen gave Jonah some protection, Dugan got soaked repeatedly from sheets of spray. The wind chill began to give him tremors.

It was the kind of night normal people would spend in bed. But they were headed toward a ship carrying the potential deaths of thousands. And, Dugan hoped, an alive Cassandra Riley. He shivered again. Adrenalin could substitute for heat for a short time, but he knew he shook not only from the cold now.

Chapter 29

Hanging onto the leaping console, Dugan pulled out the cell phone he took from the Admiral's Arms and tried to make out the keys in the dark as the boat pounded up and down. His mind was numb, and he tried to force his brain to function, to remember the open-line number for Sal. He tried twice and got busy signals.

Finally, Jonah saw what Dugan was struggling with. He slowed the boat down, pulled the flashlight from its locker, and steered one-handed while he focused the light on the keyboard. The slower speed and extra light gave Dugan the chance he needed to get the call through. With one arm looped through the support, Dugan braced his feet and pressed the phone to his ear as Jonah hit the throttles again. After the first ring, Sal came on in his usual, calm style.

"Where the hell are you?" No preamble, no "are you okay?" He would have talked to Chin by now, and the rest of the staff would be putting the whole picture together for him.

Dugan wondered briefly what kind of pandemonium was going on in the ops center, but Sal spoke as calmly as if they were discussing a football game. "The SEAL takedown didn't happen," Sal said. For a moment, hanging onto the plunging boat in the freezing water, Dugan remembered the explosions and the big, self-confident SEAL commander at the planning sessions who was sure this would be something his SEALs could handle. Maybe he'd survived.

Dugan didn't know where the cell network he was using came from or how long the connection would last. The drones were iffy; maybe the weak commercial system had kicked in, or maybe the cell system the bad guys put up still worked at this distance. *To hell with security,* flashed through his mind. *I need to call the cavalry.*

"I'm on a boating adventure," Dugan yelled, briefly describing the scene—Jonah at the controls, the boat, the direction they were moving. He hung on for dear life and ground the phone into his ear to hear over the roar of the engine. Behind him and to the right, he could make out the distant lights around the old Walker place, where the troops were rounding up the surviving bad guys and the former hostages. Dugan figured Chin had medics, but there would shortly be more ambulances, doctors, and cops around Brewer than anybody could ever need.

Apparently, the drones were not all down. "I think we have you," Sal said in a flat, unemotional voice, though Dugan noticed he spoke louder, as if Sal appreciated the slamming and soaking he was getting. "Your target is zero-four-five degrees from your present direction of travel at about a mile."

"Hang on," he said into the phone. Waving his arm at Jonah, he pointed roughly forty-five degrees to the right and yelled, "One mile!"

The big vet nodded, and the boat began a sweeping curve, changing the direction of the waves and sending water sheeting over the port side. Spray burst back from the bow and lashed across Dugan's face.

"So what do you think?" asked Sal.

"I think we're going to board that bastard. At a minimum, we might be able to stop the go-fast." He did not mention Cassandra, since Sal was juggling bigger problems. "Anyway, I think we should give it a try."

There was an uncharacteristically long silence from Sal when Dugan finished. Sal gave a lot of rope to agents at the scene, but what Dugan proposed was a shocker even to Sal. For the first time in their long career together, Sal couldn't be sure Dugan would obey anyway. Sal knew Dugan's black dog, and it was showing now.

"You understand this is a long shot," he said.

Dugan nodded silently in the roaring darkness, forgetting Sal couldn't see him. But the man sensed Dugan's agreement.

"We are going to use the other agencies of government we talked about, and you are going to risk winding up as collateral damage." There was a pause.

The rain came down hard, the spray sheeted over the bow and visibility was a joke. Jonah was still pounding the boat, throttle wide open, charging like the Light Brigade in the direction Dugan had indicated, straight toward a black wall. In the darkness, the slam of the blunt bow through the swells threw up water that was almost phosphorescent. Dugan's knees hurt from the pounding of the flat-bottomed skiff on the waves.

"You know you're putting your ass in a vise," Sal said, which for him was a huge step away from his normal clipped style. "The weather is getting so bad we can't count on overheads or much else. I will try to convince our... ah, superiors that you should have one more shot, but if the ship moves closer to higher-value targets, then we have to do what we have to do."

He let that sink in. "If they have the devices on board, they don't have to get much further. Any detonation is a national disaster."

While Sal talked, Dugan dropped to his knees after a particularly violent collision with the building waves. As he struggled to regain his footing, he saw the loom of something huge just ahead. Phone forgotten, Dugan motioned frantically to Jonah to

168

cut the throttles. He could have saved himself the effort. Jonah saw it at the same instant, and even as Dugan waved his hands in the darkness, the vet savagely chopped the throttles all the way back.

The sudden loss of power was like hitting a brick wall. Dugan lost his grip and slammed into the bottom of the boat, skidded, and tumbled to the bow. The 9mm in his hip pocket dug painfully into his side, and the phone fell into the water sloshing around inside the hull. Jonah, braced against the stand-up console, did better and kept control. But as the boat approached the massive, dark wall of steel, the lee of the looming ship sheltered them, and the effect of the wind dropped dramatically.

They had become so accustomed to the howl of the wind that its cessation was startling. The smaller boat's momentum drifted them forward, and the massive steel side made its own eddies and currents. With the throttles cut, the tossing boat lost way and surged toward the larger vessel towering above them, huge, menacing, and cold. Their bow pinged against the metal, then pulled away as Jonah, his hands gentle on the throttle, idled quietly in reverse to get away from the suction of the massive hull. Ten feet away, they lay surging gently in the chop while the *thrum-thrum* of the ship's diesel vibrated through the water, their boat's hull, and into the soles of their feet.

Against odds, they had found the ship, and even more surprising, the people on board didn't seem to know they were there. The cell phone was gone. Sal and his problems were out of reach now. Dugan scuttled back to the console, creeping unsteadily in the wildly rocking skiff, conscious of the wall of steel just a few feet away.

"Jonah," he said as softly as he could and still manage to be heard, "the sonofabitch stopped."

"Yeah," Jonah said. His face was hidden by darkness, but the fighting madness was still there. Dugan could feel it in him and in himself.

169

"This is the mother ship," Dugan said. "The go-fast has to be around here. Let's find it."

Jonah nodded and moved the gearshift but left the engines in their near-silent, slow-stroke idle. The little boat steadied on a course parallel to the ship's side and began to move forward in the surging waves, while the towering hull served as a windbreak against the nor'easter. They seemed to be edging away from the low-vibration pulse of the ship's engine. They moved slowly, engine idling, the black wall of steel on their right.

Dugan heard them before he saw them. Voices in the darkness, the sound of metal striking metal, another engine muttering and sputtering in the dark. And then, coming slowly into view in the rain and the gloom, the stern of the go-fast boat from the boathouse, a line leading up onto a recessed cleat in the ship's side. There would be a line at the bow too, Dugan knew. She was tied up alongside waiting to receive her cargo for delivery further up the Potomac.

There was no time to think or plan. Dugan put his mouth against Jonah's ear. "I'm going to board the go-fast, drop anybody on it, turn it loose, and then go up on deck. All I want you to do is put me alongside. Then you take off."

Jonah didn't say a word but did his magic with the throttle and nudged the boat up to the stern of the go-fast. The bigger boat's deck was two feet higher than the little skiff, allowing them to approach unseen by the two figures in the boat's bow who were concerned with something in the cockpit.

Dugan steadied himself in the smaller boat, then when a wave lifted both, he scrambled up and over the stern of the more stable go-fast and approached the deckhands from behind in the darkness. He clipped one man beside the ear with the 9mm, and the man dropped. But when the speedboat banged abruptly against the side of the ship, Dugan slipped and fell on the rolling deck. He landed hard on his back, knocking the wind out of him.

A second man lunged with a flash of a knife toward Dugan's midsection. Dugan rolled to one side, struggling to get to his feet on the pitching deck. The attacker landed heavily where Dugan's prone body had just vacated. And stayed there.

In the dark, Dugan saw the loom of Jonah's bulk, the flash of his eyes.

"Turned the skiff loose," he said. "Might as well stick around. Looks like you're going to take some looking after."

Dugan drew a ragged breath. "If you insist."

They were now aboard the boat that carried Cassandra away. He tried not to think of where she might be once these people didn't need her for a shield. Dugan jammed the 9mm into his rear pocket, then searched the unconscious man, removing a pistol and an extra clip. He passed both to Jonah.

"Here. In case you can't use the shotgun where we're going." He looked forward. "Let's check this thing out."

A quick search above and below decks didn't turn up anybody else.

"We kill the engines, cut this thing loose, and go up the ladder," Dugan said.

Jonah's eyes rolled upward, but he nodded and moved to the control console. Dugan found the throttle and pulled it back. Jonah hit the kill switch and stopped the engine. Dugan ripped the key from the ignition and threw it overboard while Jonah opened the engine compartment and went to work.

Dugan couldn't see Jonah's hands, but he knew Jonah would know what to do. For his part, after feeling under the dash, Dugan ripped out the ignition wires, so jazzed on adrenalin that they came away like cheap cotton string.

Jonah finished in the engine compartment. "Tore out the spark plug wires," he said with satisfaction. "Take a mechanic and lots of spare parts to make this thing run again."

"Okay, up the ladder," Dugan said.

In the darkness, a rope pilot's ladder hung down the side of the ship and rested just above the motorboat's deck. The go-fast pitched and rolled against the side of the ship, fiberglass on metal, the screeching complaint subdued against the roar of the waves and the howl of the wind. Jonah moved to the ladder, one hand still gripping the shotgun, and began to climb.

Dugan moved to the bow of the speedboat and released the bowline from the cleat, then moved as quickly as he could manage to the stern on the bucking deck without going over the side. The stern line wasn't properly cleated, and the landlubber's tangle of knots took him precious seconds to release while the motorboat drifted away from the ship's side. Dugan ran back to the middle of the boat and leaped for the rope ladder now banging against the steel plates impossibly far away.

With his legs in the water and his arms straining with his weight, he hooked onto the ladder.

Chapter 30

The president's national security advisor wore suspenders and shirtsleeves, and there were cups of cold coffee around the Situation Room along with the remains of a sandwich buffet along the wall. Here at the summit, there were no ringing phones and no crowds of aides or action officers. Occasionally someone opened a door and the buzz of voices intruded, but only for a moment. Here there were only people who made the decisions, who had elected to stay in the target city.

The president was gone, evacuated as planned, and around the city, escorts quietly rounded up key members of congress and moved them to sites long designated for this sort of emergency. Some cabinet officers were evacuated; the ones who were working the crisis were in the situation room, and there was no thought of leaving.

Silence settled in the room as the loss of the SEAL boats sank in. Winstead now stood at the head of the table, dominating the room.

"How many?" Winstead asked, his face bleak.

"Forty SEALs that we know of," the director of the CIA said.

"Forty. My God."

"The ship evidently mounted armament we didn't anticipate. The boats were sunk or heavily damaged. There are people in the water. We'll get to them."

The chief of Naval Operations opened his mouth to speak, then closed it. It was the CIA's mission, and the admiral was going to let it play out.

The CIA director went on with a nod to the impassive CNO. "The naval option is now out. We held back any other naval assets to avoid warning the target ship. That was my decision. There are no combatant ships close enough to overhaul the freighter in time, even assuming they would win the missile fight. I recommend going for the air option."

He paused. "We may have a man on the ship."

Winstead's eyes widened. "We have a man on board? How did that happen? Was that in the plan?"

"No. He was supposed to be on the shore, leading the SEALs in. But we think he got out to the ship. We're not sure how."

Winstead picked up the phone that connected him to the president, now en route to his designated safe location.

"Mr. President, Sal—Agent Leoni—says he thinks that the man who led the SEALs into the hostages may have gotten on the ship. He's apparently very resourceful. But we have a ship with at least one nuclear weapon, probably two, just downriver from two major US cities. Our first plan has gone seriously wrong, and right now there's nothing between that weapon, or weapons, and two U.S. cities but a little distance and a big storm. We are going to execute the backup options we've planned."

The president didn't hesitate. "I agree. Do it."

Harvey Winstead set down the telephone and turned back to the room.

~

Dugan didn't know how long he hung there by his arms; it felt like eternity. His whole world was surging up and down, and he was freezing. The water was nearly up to his waist, and the waves broke over his head, trying to tear him from the ladder.

When the waves pushed him into the ship, his legs scraped against the rough plates, and then she rolled away, and he hung suspended half-in, half-out of the water from the rope ladder. His arms trembled. He had no strength, and the black water pulled at him.

The rungs on the pilot's ladder were broad wooden steps, eight inches across, that stood out from the ship's side. With the last of his strength, Dugan heaved himself up, sobbing with the effort. A surge of water against the ship's side helped him get one knee and then the other on the bottom step as another wave broke over his head, submerging him completely. The ladder swung away from the ship again, smashing him back into the steel hull, nearly breaking his grip. But now he kneeled on the ladder, arms locked into the ropes, head pressed against the third step. As he fought for his life, he dimly felt Jonah moving up the swaying ladder above him.

"Hey, man." Dugan heard Jonah's hoarse whisper. "You goin' hang there all night?"

Dugan drew a breath, trying to push away the fear. "No, just catching my breath." He took another ragged gulp. The darkness receded. He had never been so afraid, so close to death. Then he got a grip on himself.

"Jonah, watch your ass." He heard a chuckle from above.

"Always," Jonah answered. Dugan felt movement as Jonah's feet moved up the ladder.

Carefully, very carefully, Dugan reached up higher, took a death grip, and levered himself to a standing position on the steps. The waves now broke over his knees, and with every surge, the ladder swept away from the black hull, then crashed into it as the ship rolled, still tearing at his grip. Then he started to climb; strength came into his body as the fear fell away. After a minute the shivering stopped, and the violence of the rolls decreased as he mounted the hull.

Dugan looked back and down. The go-fast boat was nowhere to be seen. From the heaving deck in the rain and dark, the other side might not notice right away. But their speedboat option up the Potomac was gone.

That's something, Dugan thought. *The problem is halved.* He felt the weight of the 9mm against his soaking back, still there after bashing against the ship. He looked up at the ladder disappearing into the dark along the black, wet steel and kept climbing.

While Dugan climbed the ladder, Jonah was thirty feet above him and ready to board the Handy, his shotgun in his big hand. The five crewmen thirty feet away had their backs to him, focused on taking off a hatch cover. They didn't notice the big man slip over the rail and crouch behind a ventilator.

Dugan climbed heavily up after Jonah, weak and shaken, but he reached the rail without incident. The crew worked on the hatch cover as Dugan slid over the rail and crept in beside Jonah. With the wind and rain howling again across the dark decks, Dugan's soaked clothes sucked heat out of his body, and he shivered. He recognized that he was inching closer to hypothermia. They were too near the people on deck for his taste, and they both urgently needed to get out of the wind.

He tapped Jonah's arm, and they eased away from the sounds of the conversation, further back into the shadows to a sheltered spot behind some machinery. The crew's voices moved to the side of the ship and got louder. Dugan guessed they were looking down in the dark at where the go-fast boat was supposed to be. Somebody shouted something. There was the sound of running feet. And then spotlights from one of the big deck cranes came on, bathing the side of the ship in a pool of yellow light, showing the icy rain beating and splashing on the metal decks, and the ship itself rising and falling in response to the howling wind and tossing waves.

If the briefings Dugan received before the mission were right, they were aboard a medium-sized, break-bulk cargo ship, one of the most common types of the thousands of ships that carry the world's trade. She would be 300-plus feet long and have five big holds for carrying bulk cargo such as grain, coal, or most anything. The crew, under normal circumstances, would be ten to fifteen sailors, typically Filipinos, Greeks, or a polyglot mixture of seamen from the world's seafaring nations. But not tonight.

The language on deck was Arabic, and Dugan guessed at least some in the crew would have specialized skills that did not include nautical duties. The deck floodlights confirmed the speedboat the crew was about to load was missing, and they were not happy about it.

Blinking against the light, Jonah and Dugan watched from their hiding place as the crowd on the railing grew, in spite of the rain and wind whipping across the decks. Ten or twelve men stood there now, dressed in foul-weather parkas and overalls, all talking and gesturing out into the dark. A surprising number had assault rifles slung across their backs. Dugan recognized the AK-47s and -74s. He made a mental bet some of these boys hadn't spent much time at sea in the past few years. With all the yelling and gesticulating, there didn't seem to be much in the way of seamanlike behavior in this lot.

The crowd at the rail grew silent as someone approached from the general direction of the stern. As the figure moved into the lighted area of the deck, Dugan recognized the tall man from the mug shots and secret films he and Sal pored over.

Sheik Abu Husam al Din—literally Father of the Sword of the Faith—was a Saudi prince. Once an educated leader of the Saudi jet set, in the ten years or so since he'd embraced radical Islam, he and his father's fortune had become a murderous force in the shadowy world of global *jihad*. Some of his money came from the family; his father was virtually untouchable in the Kingdom. Some came from the world of human slaving, illegal drugs, or combinations of them both. For a Saudi with his contacts, money was just a lubricant that let him and his network of followers slip through the world, leaving a trail of wrecked and bloody bodies behind.

Western intelligence never actually caught up to him in the flesh. All the data came from terrified informants and mocking videos, but they knew his voice, booming out of websites and tapes, laughing, fingering the next target or the next victim with cold accuracy. Forget the murderous fanatics who live and massacre in dirt-poor places like Pakistan or what's left of Syria. Husam slipped in and out of the big cities, paying off or terrifying the politicians, living the champagne life until he disappeared again, and another bomb or assassination marked his passing. If the intelligence was right, his ambitions were growing.

Guzmann was next to him, dark and menacing as ever. But Husam was obviously in charge. Guzmann was just muscle. Husam was the complete terrorist package. The group at the rail fell respectfully silent. Dugan could feel Jonah shifting around next to him and sensed his silent questions.

The tall, handsome man with the goatee looked over the side, the hood of his parka blowing in the wind, his face impassive. Then he turned and scanned back over the ship, his eyes passing over where Dugan and Jonah lay among the winches and drums of the vessel's midships cranes. He rapped an order to a subordinate at the rail, who spoke into a two-way radio in his hand. Abruptly, the lights went out again, and the ship was covered in darkness.

We don't have much time, Dugan thought, and he began to shake again. *We've got to get below decks and out of this wind.* He gripped Jonah's shoulder once, then turned and moved as quietly as possible away from the group at the rail, keeping the cranes and deck clutter between them. He sensed Jonah moving behind him, sliding easily through the dark. They needed cover, and they needed it soon. In minutes, the ship would be crawling with hostile firepower, and Dugan wanted to find Cassandra, or at least be sure she wasn't aboard.

His chest tightened. The cold logic of his business said that pushing her up that long rope ladder was an unnecessary delay that could be easily avoided. She might have gone over the side as soon as the go-fast boat broke out of the boathouse, and she was no longer necessary. But Dugan had seen the way Guzmann looked at her, even as he turned her over to his goons to be raped and murdered, and the tall man's profile said he also had been attentive to the ladies in his pre-devout days.

If there was a chance she was alive, maybe they hadn't come all the way out here just for the ride. But there were other priorities, as well, and they were even more important. Once again, he steadied himself. *Keep your mind in the game,* flashed through his mind. *This rust bucket can kill millions.*

The first move was to get off the open deck and into shelter. With the lights off, they had a chance. Dugan moved ahead of Jonah, easing his way through the shadows toward a deck hatch that loomed faintly in the dark. As they moved, the beat of the ship's engine, slowly pulsing in the background, became louder and faster, increasing to an urgent *thrum, thrum* that vibrated through the night. There was the faintest sense of acceleration and of heeling, as if persons unknown rammed the throttle forward and put the massive ship into a turn to port.

Dugan moved at a crouch along the wet deck, feeling his way in the dark and thinking about what a turn north toward the Potomac might mean, when there was a whispering sound behind him. He turned, but not fast enough. There was a blinding flash of light, pain, and then darkness.

Chapter 31

All but the highest-flying drones were either blown off station or grounded by the weather, and the Global Hawk's infrared coverage was intermittent and hampered by cloud density as the storm blew across the Chesapeake with gusts over 40 knots. Even in the clearer periods, the ship's heat signature was oddly indistinct. Intelligence surmised that the decks were armored to dissipate the vessel's heat signature. Although the outside temperatures hovered around freezing, the thick steel around the engines and on the decks suppressed the ship's IR picture. The armor's heat suppression and the dense cloud cover made aerial detection difficult.

Sal and the Air Force general watched the big screen without expression as their technicians worked to deconflict the data pouring in from the Hawk and the AWACS.

Finally, the general turned to Sal. "We've recovered the hostages. Your man did his job. We got a hundred and sixteen people out."

Sal nodded, eyes focused on the screen.

"The other ship headed to Baltimore is out of the picture. The Coast Guard directed it to anchor. And the rescue boats are headed for the survivors of the SEAL boats. If they can stay afloat in the storm, the water's not killing cold."

Sal's face was immobile. The Handy's riposte had happened in front of their eyes, but the lousy cloud cover had dampened even the IR signatures of the explosions. Still, they were getting some information from aloft. Some comms were coming from one severely damaged boat that had remained afloat and Chin's own radios ashore, relayed through the AWACS. Chin and some of the townspeople were mounting rescue efforts from Brewer, and the Navy had high-speed boats headed for the area, although they would be an hour getting there. Sal knew all this was going on, but he had eyes only for the indistinct return on the screen; a return that wavered as the cloud cover thickened and thinned.

The general went on. "From what we can tell by a very weak IR look a few minutes ago, the go-fast delivery boat from the hostage site may have separated from the mother ship and is apparently adrift. That may be your man's work. We don't know. But the ship has begun to move. The sensors indicate it has turned up the Potomac toward Washington. If your man made it on board, I hope he stays lucky."

Sal nodded again. The general meant well, but he was really getting on Sal's nerves. "His name is Neil. Neil Dugan."

The general paused. They had worked together for days now, and he liked and admired the little man, but this was a time to be open and frank.

"Sal, you know and I know Dugan is on that ship, and maybe he can stop it by himself. But that thing has at least one nuclear device on board, maybe two, and it's starting to move up the river toward a million people in D.C. We played a very close game to even let it get this far. That was the president's call. We told him we could do it and guaranteed those boats would be stopped after we recovered the hostages. We gambled two cities against getting those people away from those bastards who were holding them. Now we have them, and we're down to one city with millions of people in the area. Game over. It's time to stop that ship."

Sal opened his mouth to speak, but an aide interrupted. Winstead was on the phone. Sal picked up.

"Sal, we're getting the same reports you are. We see two returns, an indistinct, bigger one that is probably the ship and a smaller one that is probably the go-fast.

"That's what we see. We think somebody disabled the go-fast."

"The indistinct one is turning up the Potomac," Winstead said.

"Yes. We are convinced this is the ship we've been tracking for months. It has a greatly diminished IR signature, as far as we can tell in this weather, and if our sources are right, it's got armored decks. That's probably what's stopping the IR."

"Dugan?"

"We think he's on the ship."

"Sal, we've recovered the hostages. We can't hazard a nuclear explosion in the Potomac, close to Washington or not. We can't risk it for one man."

"I understand."

"Tell your people to sink the ship." Winstead hung up.

Sal turned to the general, his face immobile. "Sink the sonofabitch."

The general nodded and looked at another officer standing by a console. "Launch," the general said.

Seconds later, two blocks away in a squadron ready room at Langley Air Force Base, the lieutenant colonel who commanded the alerted F-22 squadron turned to his pilots and reached for his flight helmet.

"Game on, folks." They left for the bus that would speed them through the rain to their waiting fighters.

~

For the second time that long day, Dugan was at the bottom of a deep, dark well. *Or maybe*, a voice said, *it's a tunnel. Hard to tell.*

He vaguely remembered being dragged down steps, thrown onto a hard deck, his hands roughly jerked behind him. Pain. Pain in his head, pain in his hands. The throbbing of the ship's engine almost synchronized with the throbbing in his head.

Thinking came hard, and it was fuzzy: pictures of dead faces and high seas and muzzle flashes. Even so, the pain was useful. He was alive, and he kept his eyes closed while feeling and sense came back. He was lying on his face, his cheek against on a rough carpet and his hands tied behind him, though his feet seemed to be free. Why wasn't he dead? He thought it over as he returned to full consciousness, his eyes still closed. The throbbing in his head receded.

Whoever hit me knew what he was doing, Dugan thought. Sensing no movement around him, he cautiously squinted one eye open and was rewarded by a glimpse of a woman's foot in a soaked hiking boot, tied to a chair leg. Something inside him relaxed a little. Without moving his head, he opened the eye all the way and was rewarded by a full view of one very wet and muddy Cassy, hair a mess but unquestionably alive. She was tied hand and foot to an armchair in what appeared to be a ship's cabin. His eye met both of hers.

Without moving his head, he grimaced what might have been a smile. Her mouth made an "O" and she straightened, and then she flashed him a big, exaggerated hey-sailor wink. He wanted to give her an exuberant, relieved hug, but there were obvious problems with that idea. Instead he made a minute movement with his head and eye, asking without speaking if anyone was around.

She shook her head the slightest, made a pursing movement with her lips and a minute nod toward the opposite bulkhead, indicating they were nearby.

He was taking this in when rising voices sounded in the passageway, and a door banged open behind him. He closed his eye.

There was a burst of Arabic. Dugan's Arabic wasn't as good as his Spanish, but he caught the words "woman" and "man." Then for a moment there was silence. He heard a step. And then someone kicked him hard in the side, just above the kidney. He woofed a breath and groaned, like someone coming out of unconsciousness.

"You see, Felix," an accented voice said in English. "He awakens."

And Dugan knew the voice, and he knew the owner.

"But not for long," said Guzmann's Spanish-accented rumble. "I do not see, *senor,* why he and the woman do not die now."

Another kick, harder still. "Because in my last hours on earth, I will indulge myself. I have come far for this, and to have an enemy share our victory will only sweeten it."

Dugan sensed a face coming close to his. "You who have no name," Husam said in a friendly, conversational tone. "I know you are listening. Awaken and talk to me." A second passed and then a third kick, not quite as hard.

Dugan groaned and opened his eyes, careful to unfocus them like a man coming out of a beating. He let a little spittle drool out of his mouth.

"He has a name," Guzmann said. "My men say he is Simpson, who calls himself a tourist." And he laughed, but it was not a nice laugh. "Many of my men have disappeared. I would know where they are. He will know more certainly than the woman." And he must have been about to kick again, but Abu Husam intervened.

Like a lot of wealthy Arabs, he spoke English with an upper-class British accent. "He is awake. Let us have a conversation."

Dugan focused his eyes slowly, acting as if he were having trouble doing it, and carefully rolled over from left to right, away from Cassandra and facing the voices, taking care to stay closed up in a loose fetal position.

"My hands hurt," he croaked. It was no acting. He grimaced. Time to reinforce the idea of a whipped dog, meek little Frank Simpson reemerging. It wasn't a hard act to pull off.

"And they will," Husam said with a smile. He and Guzmann had moved to the other side of the room, well out of range of any weak kick Dugan might try. Two Arabic-looking guys in rough clothes stood behind them, holding what looked like more H&K MP-5s.

So there are two ranks on the boat. The working stiffs who carry the AKs and the insiders with the high-speed guns, Dugan thought. These were the insiders, both big middle-easterners with hard eyes.

"And they will," Husam repeated. "But it will not trouble you for long, my friend." As he spoke, the deck tilted slightly, and there was a sense of weight toward Dugan's feet. The whole ship was pervaded with the urgent, increasing beat of the engine Dugan felt beneath their cabin. They were moving, and speed was clearly picking up.

We're in the stern, Dugan thought.

"Soon, six hours, maybe less, we will be in Washington," Husam said. "I know you hope your air force or navy will stop us before we can culminate our mission." He smiled. "It is not much of a hope."

Actually, Dugan figured that right about now, some Air Force hotshot was looking at them through a bombsight. There was no way anything floating was going to get up the Potomac tonight. The biggest risk to Cassandra and him—and to Jonah, wherever he was—was getting bombed by the Air Force or killed in a SEAL crossfire, not from the men in front of him. But Abu Husam wasn't through.

"You have caused me some inconvenience. Felix has lost many men, and for knowledge of that, we brought the lady on board." A nod in Cassandra's direction. "But she knows nothing, I am sure. Even Felix knows that now."

Felix doesn't look happy; that's a fact, Dugan thought.

"The loss of our delivery boat has forced me to change our plans, and for that and the other disruptions, I should kill you. But I admire a worthy opponent. I think instead I will let you live to see the ultimate failure of your mission, to see the end of our pilgrimage." His face glowed.

Chapter 32

Dugan knew that look from Iraq. *You just have to let them talk,* he thought. *Not that I have much choice at this moment.* Even with his hands behind him, Dugan had been able to carefully work a little slack into the ropes, and his fingers tingled as feeling came back. He could feel the gentle pressure of the knife's sheath around his calf. If he could get more play for his hands, life would be hopeful. He kept the dopey look on his face and shook his head as if trying to clear it.

"And the lady, unfortunately, will have to join us," the tall Arab said. "We do not make war on women, even your Western harlots, but there is no choice." He made a slight bow toward the disheveled and battered woman.

A gentleman to the core. And nutty as they come, thought Dugan, gently testing the knots behind his back.

"Put her ashore," Dugan croaked as Frank Simpson. "Put a life jacket on her and throw her over the side." *At least she would have a prayer.*

Husam smiled. "But my friend, perhaps she will join us in paradise. And you must see we are not stopping. Indeed, we cannot stop. This ship is operating faster now than it has ever sailed before. We are verily, ah..." He fished for the word. "...*racing* down the

187

river. The Chesapeake pilot, were he still alive, would be quite fearful. I believe we may scrape bottom several times. But still we will speed on."

He paused, as if weighing how much to say. There was a note of pride in his voice when he continued. "This ship is not an ordinary merchant ship, as it seems. It is armored against your bombs and your attacks, and the engines are very powerful. Even the steering station is below decks, where it cannot be destroyed. It is carrying the prayers of the faithful. It cannot be stopped."

So they said about the Bismarck, Dugan thought, and he decided to lead him on.

"But what do you expect to do?" he said in his best Frank-like voice. He even managed to put a little quaver in it. "What is this all *about?*"

"I've no doubt you know, Simpson or whatever your name is, we have long been planning a strike at the heart of America. This ship is the end of our planning. We who are faithful knew that the famous opportunism you are so proud of in the West would someday bring us the materiel we needed for an atomic weapon; a weapon we could use to destroy one of your great cities. We began our planning and making our preparation years before, even without the weapon itself. Surely that is notable, even in the West."

Nuttier and nuttier, Dugan thought, as he worked the ropes that bound his hands.

Husam went on. "When our Russian friends found the materiel, even enough for two devices, we were ready with plans for the delivery of the weapons. The means of destroying you and your apostate nation. We found useful allies who would assist us, here in America. Mexico is part of America, is it not?"

He smiled without warmth but with pride. "Slowly and without attracting attention, our friends in Pakistan strengthened the decks and have…" Again he paused and searched for just the right idiom. "*Souped up* the engine. It was a difficult decision, much discussed in our planning. If stealth was to bring the ship to one of your cities, why soup up the engine? But we decided it should be done to cover every chance, and tonight proves the worth of our planning. What before steamed at fifteen knots now steams at twenty-five, and the weather will make your 'smart bombs' less accurate."

He paused before going on, his face alight with pride. "Where before your bombs would easily penetrate a merchant ship, these decks are armored like a battleship against your largest munitions. This very river will frustrate your naval anti-ship missiles."

He was right, Dugan knew. The Navy anti-ship missiles were sea-skimmers and traveled several miles before they acquired their target. Even here where the Potomac was so broad, they'd have a tough time. It would have to be smart bombs from above.

For the Air Force, it wouldn't be an impossible shot, but a 25-knot ship corkscrewing up the river in a storm would be tough for anyone to hit. With the storm, the pilot would need all the electronic gadgets available to see through the weather. Even the laser-directed or self-seeker bombs might have trouble.

He remembered the confident Air Force lieutenant general at the briefing. *Hope he has better luck than the SEALs,* Dugan thought.

But Husam wasn't through. "Your famous elite forces have made their attempt, but they did not expect to find a heavily armed ship ready to fight them. A 'Q' ship, I believe the term is. The French anti-ship missiles are quite effective, even at close range. And in the hold is the prize." Once the bars were down, the words came tumbling out in his Oxford-accented English.

Dugan shifted his bloodshot eyes to Guzmann and decided to drop the quivering voice. It wasn't working anyway. "So, Felix, where do you come in on all this? You don't look like a religious nutcase." It was hard to be insulting lying on his side, with blood on his face and his hands tied, but he tried.

Husam smiled when he heard Dugan's natural voice, as if he had won a small victory.

Well, maybe he did, Dugan thought, *but the game's not over.*

Guzmann looked out of place and unhappy. Without his minions around, he seemed curiously deflated.

"*Senor* Husam has agreed to put me and my men ashore—" he began, but Husam cut him off.

"Felix, Felix," he said, putting his hand on the shorter man's shoulder. "Didn't you hear what I said to our friend here? Our plans have changed, and partly because of you and your bungling. We cannot stop for even our friends. Tonight, you too will have a vision of Paradise." He glanced quickly back at one of the impassive guards and gave an imperceptible nod.

Guzmann opened his mouth to speak, but whatever he was about to say suddenly didn't matter anymore. An explosive shot reverberated in the small cabin. He rose up on his toes as the front of his head lifted off and sailed out into the room. A splash of blood and something pink landed on Dugan's leg. Guzmann collapsed in stages, to his knees, and then onto what was left of his bloody face. A twitch and he was still.

The guard who'd fired the shot holstered his 9mm and spoke a few words into a small microphone on his headset. Dugan's ears rang, and through it, he heard Cassandra draw a shaky, sobbing breath.

Chapter 33

Thursday 0100

The four F-22s lifted off the runway at Langley and stood on their tails to gain altitude. Normally, by the time they topped 20,000 feet, they could have seen up the bay all the way to Pennsylvania, but tonight the storm and the dense cloud cover hid everything. Below them was a vast floor of gray and above them the stars burned brightly in the black sky.

"Weapons hot," said flight lead, and four sets of gloved fingers danced around the weapons suite switches. A second later, their sensors began radiating with a freedom they never would have chanced in actual air-to-air combat. But this was different. In a distant AWACS, the primary mission controller gave the flight lead a vector and the bad news: the storm below made target acquisition difficult. Faintly gray in the starlight with the tops of the storm clouds far below, the four sleek jets banked gently into a holding orbit that covered two states while they waited to be sent in. Behind them at Langley, the second flight taxied to the runway.

Dugan's wrists were looser, but still unusable. At least the blood was flowing back to his hands. He raised his head to admire Guzmann's twitching body, then dropped back onto the floor. Dropping back hurt.

"What do you want from us?" he asked, shifting his head a little to include Cassandra. *When they talk a lot,* he thought, *it's usually a good sign.* He knew Husam would give them more time. He tried not to consider that Husam had patted Guzmann on the shoulder like an old friend while his assassin drew his pistol.

The ship began a sharp turn. Dugan tried to call up a chart of the Potomac in his mind and gave up. There was no way to tell where they were.

"Us?" Husam said. He again bowed slightly toward Cassandra. "Nothing. Nothing now. I want you to remain here as my guests, both of you, while I attend to other matters. Then I will return." He rapped out some orders to his guards; Dugan caught the words "stay" and "shoot." Then he crossed the cabin into an inner passageway, leaving the two impassive gunmen watching Dugan and Cassandra, while Guzmann's body leaked over the deck.

After a long, silent minute, there were faint bursts of firing outside from several locations, then more silence. *Well, that took care of the rest of Guzmann's crew,* Dugan thought.

The ship leaned back into another turn. It was making shallow zigzags, answering the unseen helmsman. They were doing twenty-plus knots in a big ship. Way too fast for the narrow shipping channels further up the Potomac, but here near the mouth there was plenty of room. The silence was broken only by the constant thudding of the engine. He could hear Cassandra breathing behind him, but he didn't want to do anything to upset the boys with the guns.

Until, that was, the door to the passageway that Husam used eased slowly open behind the two watching them. Nobody on this suicide mission would need to be stealthy now, he realized. Without warning, he arched his back and went into a spasm, rolling his eyes and making loud gurgling sounds.

The guards wouldn't be fooled long, but he wanted their attention for a split-second. It worked. Their eyes fixed on him, and instantly the room was filled with two enormous crashes in succession. Both guards were down; their heads bloody messes and brains scattered. Blood was spattered on the walls, the carpet, and just like with Guzmann, on Dugan.

Jonah kicked the door shut, jacking another load into his 12-gauge. He warily watched one guard's body twitch aimlessly as it closed down. Then he turned to Dugan.

"Am I going to have to do this all night? Save your ass, I mean." He reached into his pocket and fed more shells into his gun.

Dugan's ears were ringing, and his voice sounded high-pitched and strained in his ears. "Untie these ropes, dammit, and try not to blow my head off with that thing. And then Cassandra."

Jonah finished reloading and cut Dugan's bonds with a pocketknife he produced from his jeans, then turned to release Cassandra. While he cut her bonds, Dugan staggered to his feet and worked his wrists to get the blood running again. His fingertips tingled.

When her ties were cut, Cassandra took a deep breath, stood, and wavered. Dugan stepped over to her and put his arm around her shoulder, which was also spattered with blood.

"Steady up," he said. "Lots to do. Can you walk?"

"Of course." She pushed away, took another deep breath, and tried not to look at the mess on the floor. The small cabin looked like a slaughterhouse. No wall was unmarked, and blood and body fluids soaked into the carpet

The deck, Dugan thought. *Got to get my terms right.* He realized he was on the edge of losing it and pulled himself together with almost a physical wrench. Grabbing one of the H&Ks, he checked the safety and tossed it to Jonah. The other he took for himself, checking the magazine and the chamber. Rolling a guard's body over, he felt around for his black pistol. He found a cell phone and slipped it into his pocket. He hefted the pistol and looked closely at Cassandra. Despite the shotgun, she'd wound up being a hostage.

"Here. A pistol this time. Any problems with shooting?"

It was a tactless thing to say, but tact was not on his mind at the moment. He needed to know who could watch his back and who couldn't.

Her eyes flashed. "About half an hour after you left, somebody outside started yelling in Spanish. The assholes started thrashing around, so I shot them like you said. Maybe they thought I wouldn't do it." She shrugged. "Two men ran in and the damned shotgun jammed. That bastard," she said pointing to Guzmann, "grabbed me and got the keys to your car out of my pocket. His hands were all over me. I never did see Deion."

Dugan nodded and said, "Deion made it. Guzmann probably wanted the government car and you to get past what was happening at the house. Well, your gun's not going to jam this time." He checked to make sure a round was chambered and the safety was on and handed it over. She took it, checked the safety herself, and turned back to Dugan.

He looked at his team of two. "Follow me."

Dugan figured the shooting should have attracted some company, but there was no alarm, only the steady thump of the ship's engine, the storm noises, and the wash of water down the ship's hull. He clicked off the light in the compartment and pushed open the steel door to the outside. A blast of freezing wind and rain smacked him in the face, while the sound of a full-blown, howling Chesapeake Bay nor'easter filled the room. Then Dugan understood why their shots hadn't attracted attention. The howling storm outside muted the noise, and the ship's crew was away on other duties.

He eased the heavy door back to a crack and looked again. Aside from the dark, ice-slick deck outside the cabin and the luminescent splatter of the icy rain, there was nothing, not even

194

ship's lights. The ship leaned into another sharp turn, and he wondered how much she would skid in those tight turns as the channel narrowed. It was icy cold.

He slammed the door, switched on the light, and turned to Jonah and Cassandra. Dugan wore jeans, a wool shirt and windbreaker, all soaked through. Jonah and Cassandra were in the same shape.

"Let's go find some foul-weather gear," Dugan said. "It's that or freeze... or stay in here until Husam or the U.S. Air Force blows us to hell."

Cassandra shuddered. Jonah looked doubtful, then nodded. Stepping over the bodies on the floor and around the pools of blood and flesh, Dugan moved across the cabin to the door leading to the passageway in the interior of the ship, the same one that Husam and Jonah had used. When Cassandra and Jonah were beside him, Dugan cut the lights and opened the door.

The door opened into a narrow, dimly lit passageway running fore and aft. It was deserted. There was a light at the far end toward the bow and a ladder that disappeared to a lower deck. In the passageway, faint imprints of Husam's bloody steps headed forward. A longer stretch reached toward the stern with a ladder at the end. Doors like the one Dugan had opened broke up the walls on either side. Two alcoves led to hatches to the outside.

Probably the way Jonah got in. He called up in his mind his sketchy briefings on this kind of ship. Sketchy because he never thought he'd actually wind up aboard. He concluded they were probably in the crew quarters aft, right above the massive engine four decks down, the target for any incoming bombs.

He pulled his head back and looked through the dimness at Jonah. "You take trail. Cassandra between us. We find an open door; we stack up and go in together fast."

Jonah nodded. He'd slung the submachine gun over his back, still favoring the 12-gauge.

Probably right, Dugan thought. He looked at Cassandra. "Okay?"

"Okay." She flashed him a strained smile and lifted the pistol.

Dugan stepped into the narrow passageway and walked boldly aft, submachine gun up. Behind him, he sensed the others. No need to skulk. If somebody came across them suddenly, an assured attitude might buy a precious half-second. Dugan walked straight to the nearest door on the other side of the passageway, yanked the handle down and pushed it open, feeling with his left hand for the lights. He flipped them on, and they piled in without hesitation. It was a storeroom with boxes and crates of canned goods. The door closed behind them.

"Nothing here," Dugan said.

"This is where I hid before I heard the shooting," Jonah said.

"Let's try again." They lined up behind him, crossed the passageway, and tried the next door. Locked. Without pausing, Dugan took a few more steps, trying the door opposite. The handle moved easily under his hand. The lights were already on when he pushed open the door.

Jackpot. The smell of unwashed bedding and bodies hit him first, then the sight of six bunks with wadded-up blankets and sheets. One seemed to be occupied by the off-watch. A bearded man blinked, rising on an elbow to protest when Jonah pounced across the cabin and jammed his shotgun muzzle into the man's face.

"You make a sound, man, I spread your fucking brains all over the wall," he hissed. Whether or not the small Arab understood English, Jonah's intention was obvious, and the man went rigid and silent.

Dugan slammed the door, twisted the locking catch, and pulled the knife from his leg sheath. He handed it to Cassandra, handle up.

"Cut up some sheets so we can tie him up and put a gag on his mouth. Hands behind him. Tight." Dugan thought for a moment. "And a blindfold." They didn't need prisoners at this stage, but he had a feeling that his two compatriots would have objected to the logical alternative.

Between Jonah and Cassandra, they made short work of their catch. He was stonily silent, staring back down the barrel of Jonah's shotgun with dark, emotionless eyes. In less time than it takes to tell, he was securely trussed, gagged, and blindfolded. Jonah pushed him into the corner, face down so he would be out of mischief.

The three yanked open the nearest lockers. The crew's trousers and shirts were nondescript and smelled of cheap soap, but they were dry. Modesty had little place in the cabin as Jonah, Cassandra, and Dugan took turns stripping out of their wet clothes and dressing in the crew trousers and shirtsleeves while someone kept an eye on their prisoner.

The foul-weather outfits were the bright red color favored by mariners the world over. They were small for Dugan and Jonah, but fine for Cassandra. In heavy jean-like trousers, a gray sweater that stank of cigarette smoke, a set of waterproof bib overalls, and a foul-weather jacket that came from the same locker, Cassandra looked like an old salt. Or at least with the hood up, she'd look enough like one from a distance to give her some protection.

Jonah was large and had to check a couple of lockers to find a foul-weather coat to pull over a dirty sweater. Dugan found a sweater and a hooded jacket like the others, but no trousers, so he kept his wet jeans and pulled on bib overalls. Boots were a failure, so Jonah and Dugan kept their wet boots. Although the search had uncovered sneakers and sea boots in Cassandra's size, she decided to keep her wet hiking boots as well.

While the others were searching lockers, Dugan pulled out the cell phone he had taken off the guard, studied it for a moment, and then dialed a number. By now they were well-out of range of whatever network they'd been using in Brewer, but evidently, they were back under general coverage.

"Six-three-two-two," the voice said. To Sal's organization, this phone was unknown. Dugan had no time for protocol.

"Your grandmother was a slut, Jimmy," Dugan said. "This is Neil. Let me speak to Sal." It was easier than remembering a password.

Sal came on the line a second later. "Where are you?"

"Three of us are on the ship," Dugan said. "We're free for the moment, and I'm thinking we'll call the captain and complain about the amenities aboard this tub."

"Where on the ship?" Sal asked sharply. "And who is 'we'?"

Even under the circumstances, Dugan smiled. He had known Sal since the farm days, and the dour little man never did have a sense of humor anyone could find, which was probably why he was where he was, and Dugan was still in the field.

"We're in the aft superstructure. We must be over the steering and the engine. Cassandra Riley and Jonah Miller are with me. Recruited help. Without them, yours truly would be toast."

Sal was silent for a second, and Dugan knew he was deciding how much to tell him.

"In about ten minutes, an F-22 from Langley Air Force Base is going to put a thousand-pound bomb about where you are now." He paused. "Or maybe sooner. They're going to take the shot as soon as they can, and I'm not sure when that will be to the second."

I'll bet not knowing is annoying the hell out of Sal, thought Dugan.

Sal went on. "Aft is no place for you to be. Get forward and under the armor, as fast as you can. The opposition has apparently abandoned the Baltimore option. Losing the go-fast boat ruined that route. That's the good news.

"Right now, you're driving up the Potomac at better than twenty knots. We're all concerned that a detonation any place would be catastrophic."

The phone connection got sketchy.

"The plan is to try to sink or destroy the ship before it penetrates any deeper into populated areas, and particularly before you reach the —"

The phone changed to static, then quit altogether. As the Handy heeled into another turn, Dugan saw clearly what he had to do, and he groaned inwardly, feeling his weariness.

Cassandra and Jonah watched him. He flipped the phone shut, gave them a follow-me wave, but as he reached for the light switch, Jonah held up his hand.

Chapter 34

"Ah, Neil, I don't want to slow us down or anything, but just what the hell is going on?" Jonah asked. "I mean, this is all very *interesting*, but you can see that it's not what we do around Brewer for fun. We got Cassandra. Let's git."

Cassandra was silent. She had heard Husam bragging. "Erin?" She asked. It was a plea.

Half of Dugan's mind was seeing the video feed from an F-22 bombsight. The crummy weather might give them a little time, but not much. He decided Jonah and Cassandra would back him up better if he told them what was going on. And if they lived or died—a coin toss at this point—he wanted these two to know what they were up against, even if it cost them their momentum.

He turned to the Cassandra. *She's got more guts than either of us. She deserves to know.* "Cassandra, I'm an agent with the Federal Bureau of Investigation."

The "with" wasn't quite a lie. It didn't seem to be the time to explain that he, Sal, and some other agents were only temporary help from another agency, sworn into the FBI for one-time use.

As he talked, the ship leaned away from another turn, shuddered, lost speed for a moment, and then seemed to accelerate briefly as she slid over the soft, muddy bottom into deeper water.

We must be getting up the river, he thought. The single screw was probably churning mud, but the bottom was soft, and the prop was unlikely to lose a blade. Dugan hadn't spent much time studying the hydrology of the Potomac, but he knew vaguely that the broad mouth of the river had plenty of depth except for the occasional shoal. Further up, the river got narrower, and depths on either side of the serpentine channel ran to twenty feet or less. He guessed that the ship probably drew a draft of a little over thirty feet, with the weight of the armor. The whole thought went through his mind in a nanosecond, and then he refocused on the task at hand.

"Erin's in good hands," he said, using the most reassuring voice he could find under the circumstances. "I saw her when we took the house down and rescued your friends—all of them. I even got a hug. Last I saw her, she was under the protection of Navy SEALs. She's safe and probably eating ice cream in some warm house right about now."

Then Dugan focused on his story, while the other part of his mind listened for the scream of a falling bomb. It was a lousy time for a dissertation, particularly with air strikes on the way.

"A year or so ago, two hundred pounds of enriched weapons-grade uranium was stolen from an old Soviet research lab. We didn't know the place even existed until after we heard that some was missing." He skipped over what had happened to the people who'd been holding it.

"We were lucky that one of the people who originally stole it came to U.S. authorities and spilled the beans. We teamed up with the Russians—that's how serious this is. We've been chasing the uranium along with every other intelligence outfit in the world ever since, but we've always been a step behind, and witnesses have been hard to find. Even before we heard of the theft from the old Soviet lab, we began to hear of a terrorist scheme to attack the U.S. by ship."

He met Jonah's eyes and the vet nodded, as if his suspicions were confirmed.

"We've known for the past year that the people who want to attack the U.S. were going to use a ship, and it started to get real when they got one and began installing armor plate below decks and working on the engine, which can't be done without talk around the waterfront. Finding all this out took painstaking, street-level intelligence work, and it was slow to get to us because sources started turning up dead."

Dugan stopped again to listen. The man in the corner was quiet. In fact, the whole ship was unnaturally silent, except for the steady beat of the engines, straining at top speed.

"Then they put the ship into normal merchant routines, and we lost it among all the other things we were trying to keep track of. We figured they wanted to use the ship to enter the Chesapeake and use the bay and the Potomac as a route to hit two big targets. One was Baltimore; the other was Washington—the real gem. But to get up the Potomac, they needed a smaller boat. So they went looking for a go-fast boat with lots of speed and good range, and somebody from shore to meet the ship. To solve the problem, they hired a Mexican drug gang; that's where our late friend Guzmann came in. The Zetas bought the boat in Florida and then drove it up the Intercoastal Waterway.

"But the gang needed a base for the boat that would give them a lot of leeway on timing; ships can't always keep exact schedules. They decided to find a small place on the bay, close to where the ship and the speedboat would rendezvous, where they could hide the boat for a few days and be under the radar. Brewer fit perfectly."

"So they moved in," Jonah said.

"Yeah," Dugan said. "It was just right. Brewer was easy to isolate. Once they'd met the ship and the deal was done, they would leave. I don't know if they'd have killed everybody or not. Probably they would have. Cassandra was certainly in the crosshairs."

She met Dugan's eyes, and he thought of the scene in the Admiral's Arms. For a moment he hesitated, then went on. "But the explosion would cause such an uproar in the country that a few dead people in Brewer wouldn't even be a blip on the news until much later."

"Those shitheads. Now what?" Cassandra said.

"When we got rid of the speedboat, Abu Husam made a decision," Dugan said, listening harder. He wanted to move and move fast. "He's decided to use this ship to drive for the prize itself." The ship lurched into a left-hand zig, shuddering with the rudder effort and throwing them all against the bulkhead.

"We've got to move, and you're not going to like the next part." They both looked at Dugan deadpan, as if nothing he could say now would matter.

"This ship is a floating bomb, but not just any kind of bomb." In the distance he heard a muted explosion, and he made a bet with himself that an F-22 pilot had tried a smart bomb that missed in the fog and rain. There were shouts outside in the passageway and somebody ran by.

God, Dugan thought, *we have to move.* The ship began the zag, and they braced themselves against the turn.

"Somewhere down below are a couple of nuclear devices. Right now, you're on a ship that is on a suicide mission to take out Washington. I think the Air Force is going to try to blow us to little pieces. In fact, I think they just took a shot and missed. The next jet is probably on its bomb run right now. But with the weather the way it is, they may not make it before the nukes are triggered.

"You heard Husam talk about armor under the decks. The engines and the armor may let them drive this thing close enough to the D.C. area to kill a million people. Even if they don't make it all the way to the city, a nuclear detonation will kill people with the blast and downwind radiation." Dugan paused to give Jonah and Cassandra time to catch up.

"I don't think the Air Force will get them in time. I think Husam will blow the bomb, or bombs, when he thinks we're close enough. We're all there is. We've got to find the bombs and disarm them."

Jonah was silently mouthing curse words.

Cassandra recovered first. "Well, it's not much for a first date, but you sure aren't boring." She gave Dugan a lopsided grin that made him want to kiss her.

Hell of a place to find romance, he thought.

"Jesus, yes," Jonah said, then he also grinned. "Well, it'll make a damn good story. Let's be about the Lord's work."

Chapter 35

The F-22 flight lead bored through the clouds on the first pass. He wasn't concerned about the darkness outside his canopy or the storm winds he passed through; his instrumentation and the AWACS gave him excellent situational awareness. But his target-seeking infrared radar was giving him indefinite returns, and the fuzzy fix he thought was the ship was not returning the kinds of data he needed for a sure hit.

But the general had said to take the shot, no matter what. The pilot unshackled the fire control system to do its job. The plane's internal computers calculated a release point, showed the bomb's internal seeker where it thought the target was, opened the bay doors, and the Joint Direct Attack Munition, or JDAM for short, was pushed by hydraulic arms into the slipstream. In less than a second, the sequence completed, the bay doors slammed shut, and the F-22 banked steeply away to the left, accelerating as it climbed toward the top of the cloud cover.

Immediately, the inertial guidance system of the JDAM attempted to steer the 1000-pound bomb toward the target it had lodged in its brain. But the plot had been indefinite, and it was moving erratically. Using its onboard GPS and the small control fins on the tail of the bomb, the brain tried to follow the fuzzy target as the JDAM dropped through the storm's turbulence. In good weather, the JDAM has a ten-meter circle of accuracy. In this case, at the last minute, the brain fixed on a spot in the water a quarter-mile from the speeding ship and detonated out of the channel in twenty feet of water.

The flight lead was already in the starlight as his wingman bored in on her own run. Like the lead pilot, she faced the same indefinite firing solution. She felt the fighter shudder momentarily as the JDAM was pushed out, and she started her pullout. There were four planes, and they had three JDAMs apiece. They were sure to hit eventually, and now that lead had taken the first shot, they could pick up the pace.

Behind her, the third F-22 had already begun its run. At Langley, the second F-22 flight, armed with more bombs, began to move down the rain-swept runway. In seconds, they were climbing almost vertically, and second flight lead was listening to the AWACS vector them to a holding pattern.

Chapter 36

Dugan grinned at both of them. The Lord's work? Well, why not?

"Done," he said, flipping up his hood. He crossed to the steel door opposite the one they had come in. The captive made a weak effort to kick out at Dugan as he passed. Without breaking stride, Dugan stomped his ankles hard. The bound man let out a muffled howl around the gag, then was quiet.

Dugan hit the light switch and plunged them all into darkness, then undogged the heavy door to the outside. As before, he was pushed back and partly blinded by howling wind and sleet, but this time at least, he had a hood. He stuck his head into the gale and looked fore and aft. He saw only darkness, and no movement save for the surging and hissing of the water along the hull. For a second, he thought he saw lights on shore, still distant. The river had not yet begun to narrow as dramatically as it would in a few more miles upstream.

He motioned Cassandra and Jonah on deck, gestured them to places along the bulkhead, slammed the big door shut, and turned the latching dogs to keep it closed. Then Dugan turned on the lurching deck to his two companions, put his back to the wind, and pulled their two hooded heads down close to his.

He had to shout above the wind. "First, we gotta get the hell away from the back of the ship, from the Air Force's aiming point."

They nodded.

"Let's go to the hatch they opened. That's probably where the first bomb is. Then we've got to have a way to get out. Follow me." He released them and started working his way up the deck, straight into the thirty-knot wind, hood blowing back and ice now stinging his face and rattling off his borrowed foul-weather jacket.

No one was on the dark deck, and the icy wind lashed the glistening steel in sheets. The river was still wide enough at this point that waves were breaking at the ship's side and throwing spray as high as the rails. The three of them were abruptly thrown against the ship's superstructure as the ship vibrated and skidded through another turn to port. Dugan lurched off the bulkhead, and with the others following him, began hand-over-handing their way along a grab rail toward the center of the ship as rapidly as they could move against the wind. Dugan didn't expect to find anybody on deck, and the steering station would be somewhere under armor belowdecks.

Stumbling, and at times crawling on their knees, across the open spaces on the deck, they made it to nearly midships, past the first two hatches away from the aft superstructure and under one of the big cranes. Then Dugan stumbled on something soft. With all his alarm bells going off, he dropped with one knee into a man's stomach and stopped the killing chop just in time when he realized he was looking at a corpse. The stare from the frozen face was long past seeing him or anyone, ever.

One of Guzmann's, he thought. In the darkness Dugan could just make out the blood frozen on his chin and chest where the submachine's bullets hit him. Dugan straightened up and moved on, the other two following him silently, scarcely pausing at the lump on the deck. *Well,* he thought, *compared to what they've seen already, one more dead man or two isn't worth much attention.*

As they crept along, the part of Dugan's brain that wasn't iced over was trying to think through the next move. Staying on deck would be useless. Trying to assault the wheelhouse and run the ship aground wasn't practical. Not only was the ship almost certainly being steered from a secure compartment, but sooner or later, a big bomb was going to come down the stack, through the roof, or whatever, and blow the stern to smithereens. The Air Force would eventually get the range. He looked up and aft at the dimly lit ports on the bridge. *Nope, not going up there,* he thought.

As long as they stayed on deck, there was a good chance of not seeing anybody, Dugan decided. The only reason Husam would put people on deck would be to look for them, and it was more than possible the terrorist didn't yet know they had gotten loose. If Husam did send people outside to look for them, Dugan's bet was he wouldn't turn on the deck lights, since the hard-core thugs left aboard would probably be equipped with night-vision goggles anyway. And turning on the lights might help the good guys. Even though fighter aircraft had great night-vision bombsights these days, darkness and storm might still be some kind of cloak.

Because the ship's steering gear and engine were protected under armor, Dugan knew Husam's best option was to take the punishment and drive the ship as far upriver as she would go. The nukes were under armor too, and even if he couldn't get under the Woodrow Wilson Bridge south of Washington itself, a near miss downriver around Fort Belvoir or the Marine base at Quantico would kill a lot of people and would be a propaganda stroke that would rock the world. Husam was probably hunkered down below, planning to detonate the nukes when he had gone as far as he could go.

So obviously they should go below too, Dugan decided, for a lot of reasons. One was they were freezing. Two was they needed the protection of the armor. And three, the bombs would be under the armor too, and they had to go below decks to find them.

The downside was that would also be where the bad guys and all their guns were. Dugan tried to do a quick calculation, but there was no way to tell if Husam had ten men on board or a hundred. He was on a suicide mission, and Dugan had no feel at all for how many sailors or assorted triggermen would volunteer to accompany him to Paradise. From Husam's point of view, now that the game was up, with a dedicated crew and a competent steersman, there was really not much left to do but crank up the engine all the way, go below, and prepare for the seventy-two virgins.

While Dugan mulled his options, they moved amidships on the port side. Near the third hatch, against the base of one of the cranes, he found what he was looking for—a large, squarish, metal box about twenty feet from the ship's side with a top slanted toward the rail. A simple, levered catch held the top closed. Dugan grabbed the lever, popped the top open, and reached inside. Again, his hand hit something soft, but this time it was good news. The life jackets were neatly stacked and ready, per international seafaring regulations. He let the lid down softly and again pulled the two others close.

"This is our way out—" he started, and then there was a blinding flash of light, a thunderous crash, and the ship shuddered from aft. A big bomb, right on target, went straight through the bridge. After the flash, there was nothing else; no flame, no subsequent explosions. Dugan's guess was anybody in the deckhouse was dead. From where they were, he couldn't see what was left of the superstructure, but there was no slackening of the steady beat of the ship's engines, and he didn't feel any loss of speed. The bomb had hit armor and hadn't penetrated. Jonah swore to himself again. Cassandra was silent.

"Air Force," Dugan said, unnecessarily. "Trying to sink us. They'll try again. The life jackets are our way out." He explained what was on his mind. If the bloody ship sank under them, they'd meet at the life jacket locker and go over the side together. When he finished, Jonah and Cassandra nodded, though he couldn't tell if it was really agreement, or just what-the-hell acquiescence. He had no thought that it would work, since they were far more likely to be bombed by the Air Force, shot by the crew, or blown to atoms by a nuclear bomb and a *jihad*-happy nutcase. But believing there was a way out would be a comfort to anybody who survived. He hoped Cassandra or Jonah would; they hadn't signed up for this.

But now they had to get off the deck. Another bomb was probably on the way. For a moment, his mind's eye pictured an F-22 above the clouds, reaching down with its radar sight and a smart bomb to get a target solution on the weaving ship. Bad weather would hurt accuracy, though not by much, and the ship's movement might make them take longer to aim. That bomb might have been just a lucky shot. The wind continued to howl across the deck as the ship heeled.

Dugan lost his balance and staggered and skidded on ice toward the rail. He dropped to the deck, catching a deck stanchion, but as he recovered his balance, a muffled *karump* sounded off the port side. A geyser of black water rose from the river close by and cascaded across the deck, driving Dugan and the others to their knees by the weight of the almost-freezing water.

Strike two, Dugan thought. *Fifty feet to the right and we'd have been on the bulls-eye.* He looked back at his companions, who were getting to their feet with some difficulty. *We've got to get below.*

Lurching and staggering, he led the way across the deck to midships. A hooded hatchway that gave momentary shelter from the wind loomed out of the dark. There was no time for caution. Dugan got to the door ahead of Cassandra and Jonah and grabbed the latching dogs. Jonah thudded up beside him, and together they heaved on the big handles, first at the top of the hatch and then at the bottom. To Dugan's infinite relief, the heavy steel door swung outward, helped by a surge of the ship to starboard.

As they clustered around the hatch, a dim red light came from the decks below. There wasn't any conversation or hesitation as they stepped over the raised steel sill and into the ship.

Chapter 37

The second F-22 pilot was reasonably sure she'd gotten a hit, and she smiled in her oxygen mask as she screamed into a six-G climbing turn to the left, accelerating toward the tops of the clouds. She always felt this way when the plane's 35,000 pounds of thrust drove her upward. She was exhilarated, even transported as she guided the plane almost vertically toward the stars.

There was nothing like it, not sex, not anything she ever knew. And this was the real thing. She knew the stakes and was willing to drive her plane into the ship if that was what it would take. She knew her fellow pilots felt the same way. Her warrior's heart sang as she broke out of the clouds into the starlight, her engine thundering behind her.

~

Jonah slammed the big door shut behind them and clicked the latches as he dogged the door from the inside. Although there were still plenty of ship noises, the sudden loss of the howling wind was startling. In the dim light, Dugan snapped the safety off the submachine gun he carried and went down the steel steps a few feet to a steel-grate landing, then paused to let the others catch up.

Below them, falling away to a dimly lit, cavernous space three stories deep, was the third cargo hold of the ship. Twenty feet down, a bare steel deck faded into the distance. A ladder ahead of them⋅ dropped to the deck below, passed through a hatch opening, then disappeared into the darkness of the lower part of the cargo hold. The weak red light illuminating the ship's ribs and skeletal deck frames cast deep shadows and stark edges in the depths. It could have been a scene from Hell.

Forward, a brighter glow on the deck indicated human activity. The steady beat of the ship's engines continued to pound with a slightly strained sound, like they were performing at speeds higher than they were designed for.

Well, Dugan thought, *this is a one-way trip. No need to change the oil.* The empty hold meant the ship was riding high, all the better to slide over the mud in the turns.

Dugan thought fast. If there were two bombs and they had been planning to load one on the speedboat, then one would still be on the upper deck of the midships cargo hold, ready to be hoisted over the side. If Dugan's guess was right, then the nuclear bomb was on the deck ahead of them. Dugan glanced back at Cassandra, caught her eye, and pointed to the landing they stood on and made a sitting motion and the universal signal for watching, pointing to his eyes with two fingers, then spanning them across the room.

She nodded, backed up to the top of the steps just under the hatchway, and settled back with her pistol in her hand. Jonah handed her his black submachine gun, safety off. She nodded, put the pistol down, and laid the spray gun across her lap. Then with Jonah and his shotgun a few feet behind, Dugan began to move down the steel steps with his submachine gun, muzzle pointing forward.

The heavy beat of the engine, the lurching and swaying of the ship, the steps and the deck as she skidded through another turn, and the dim red glow of the below-decks lighting system all combined to make the place seem unearthly and surreal. With their hoods up, they resembled heavily armed medieval monks, but Dugan hoped they looked like everybody else, at least until they got close. He could feel the heat coming up from belowdecks. Bundled up as they were, they would be sweating in minutes.

Dugan's feet hit the steel mesh of the first deck just as the ship shuddered and wrenched sideways, and an earsplitting explosion drove both men to their knees. Up ahead in the gloom there was a flash of light, briefly seen, and then smoke rolled toward them in a thick, suffocating cloud as one of the JDAMs exploded near the bows and ripped open the first crack in the ship's armor.

Dugan staggered to his feet and suddenly had company as four figures erupted from the gloom behind him and ran past, toward the forward part of the ship. In the confusion of the explosions, they didn't have time to spare for their two fellow crewmen. Dugan glanced back, caught the flash of Jonah's eyes in the haze, and followed the four along the steel deck forward, toward a glow in the distance, a bright spot that turned out to be a crowd of about five of the crew grouped around a large silver metal packing case, securely lashed down to recessed cleats on the deck and positioned under what appeared to be the hatch.

We guessed right, Dugan thought, as he caught a glimpse through the smoky haze of a rectangular open frame in the deck above with rain and storm coming in. *Hatch is still open,* he realized as he felt the rain on his face. For a split-second Dugan contemplated what an armor-piercing 1000-pound guided bomb would do if it found this chink in the ship's armor. The five crewmen were milling around the crate as if to protect it, shouting excitedly to each other, growing alarmed by the acrid smoke blowing back.

The trip to paradise wasn't supposed to be like this, Dugan thought. So intent were they on each other that they never saw Jonah and Dugan until their gun muzzles guns began to flash.

The two cut them down without mercy or remorse. The burst from the submachine gun and the boom of Jonah's shotgun cut sharp edges in the general maelstrom of engine noises and the ship's labored passage through the water. Taken by complete surprise, the five collapsed like marionettes with cut strings. One moved as if to rise, then fell still.

Dugan and Jonah crouched beside the container on opposite sides to face return fire, the rain filtering down from above, but there was no reaction from within the ship. Jonah moved to Dugan's side, gun up, watching both forward and back toward the hatchway to the lower deck as he fumbled for more buckshot to feed into his 12-gauge. Leaning his H&K against the shiny steel case, Dugan looked it over.

It appeared to be a standard six-by-eight-foot commercial shipping container with slightly bigger than ordinary latches. Dugan saw no sign of wires or drill holes where there shouldn't be, but there wasn't a lot of time for careful analysis.

A padlock securing the lid was opened. He popped the two heavy-duty latches on the long side, then the two on each end. He threw the top back and winced. No boom, no flash, no explosion. He glanced at Jonah, whose face glistened in the red dimness. His attention seemed to be wholly fixed on the lower-deck hatchway. Dugan hoisted himself up and dropped inside.

The experts who briefed Sal and Dugan had made some informed guesses about what the bomb would look like. Dugan inwardly acknowledged how right their guess had been as he examined the steel casing laying in the sawdust packing.

From what Dugan could tell, they'd used an old steel cylinder for the tube and even polished it up. The ends were welded shut, but out of the nearer end was a mechanism that looked vaguely like the bolt action on an old-time rifle without the bolt, slanted down into the cylinder, with some wires leading back to a clacker grip, like on a U.S. Claymore mine.

216

Put a blasting cap in the slot, push it down the reamed-out barrel into the cylinder amid the explosive charge, close the clacker's grip quickly, and the mechanism generates just enough electricity to fire the blasting cap, which in turn explodes the propellant into the first subcritical mass, which drives it forward. There goes most of a city. Dugan followed the wires from the old rifle barrel and saw the clacker wedged in the sawdust next to the cylinder, wires clamped to the connectors on the dull green box. The wire bail that prevented the handle from closing was pushed out of the way. *The safety's off,* he realized with a chill. *This thing's ready to go.*

No time to think. Without wasting motion, he set the safety on the clacker, pushed the two release clips to disconnect the firing wires from the generator handle, and separated them by a foot or more to minimize the risk of stray static electricity. Then he very slowly and gently began pulling on both wires to draw out the blasting cap. The little silver tube came out of the old barrel and slid easily into his hand. He realized he'd been holding his breath the whole time.

He stuck his head up to check on Jonah and was just about to make a witty comment when there was a blinding flash of light, a deafening explosion, and the world that was the ship shuddered and bucked down its length. Where the portside rail should be on the deck above was a gaping hole. The Air Force's aim was improving, but Dugan felt the throb of the engines still, remorselessly driving the hull forward. He climbed over the side of the packing case like a ninety-year-old, grabbed Jonah, and shoved his mouth next to the vet's ear.

"That's one," he said against the howling and throbbing racket on the deck. "The other one must be lower down." He moved around the packing crate, lifted the hinged lid, and pushed the cover back on the crate. Then he snapped the four latches down to reseal the crate, and for good measure, retrieved the discarded padlock and used it to lock the top. He still held the blasting cap by its wires.

"Man, this is crazy!" Jonah said. "We goin' to get our asses either sunk or blown away." But Dugan noticed he never took his eyes off the hatch to the lower deck.

"We got the case closed up against a bomb strike," Dugan yelled above the din. "Don't need a thousand-pounder setting off the explosive charge." He moved toward the hatch. "I gotta go down there. You still in?"

Jonah glanced at him. "You paying for overtime?"

"Double what you're getting now."

"I'm in," the big man said. "But I sure don' like dark places."

"No cure, but it might not be dark long." He motioned at the rent in the deck above their head.

They headed toward the bow and forward hatch, Dugan still carrying the blasting cap. With Jonah watching his back, they headed together into the smoky red gloom, under a deck perforated here and there by the best ordinance in the Air Force inventory. Dugan sensed that, though the beat of the ship's engine hadn't slowed, she might have been a little sluggish going into the last turn.

Was she taking on water? We must be well up the river, but the depths in the channel here are still deep enough to sink her. She might hang up on a sandbar in the turns, especially if she's filling with water and taking more depth.

~

By now, eight F-22s were stacked up and more were coming off the Langley runways. The first flight was halfway through its bomb load, and the pilots were sure they were getting hits, but the weather was so bad that damage assessment was almost impossible. Air traffic control was getting complicated, and at various stages of the still-secret operation, tempers began to fray. Where it counted though, there was still calm.

Sal and the general stood in the center of the operations cell, though now it was the general who made decisions and tallied results. But even the general didn't know with certainty if they were having any effect. The ship was still making knots up the Potomac. Now that the news was out, the Navy sortied an Arleigh Burke-class destroyer from Norfolk, and she steamed northward at thirty-five plus knots, overmatching the freighter nearly sixty miles ahead, but she would never catch up before the freighter got close to the Washington area.

Considering the stakes, the Situation Room was quiet as Winstead and others watched the life-and-death duel in eerie silence. From what Winstead could tell, stopping the Handy was up to the Air Force and the F-22s. The flat screen on the wall showed the infrared feed from the Global Hawk. The picture was unbroken green clouds with an occasional greener, pencil-thin streak across the screen to indicate an aircraft on a bombing run.

Winstead broke the silence twice to answer calls from the president, but he had little to tell him. Outside, operations officers were monitoring the chatter of the pilots and the AWACS operators, but after several minutes, the chairman of the Joint Chiefs ordered that fragmentary reports not be brought into the room. Just report complete facts, the operators were told. And they had none. The storm was so ferocious, they couldn't even locate the target.

The director of Homeland Security whispered for a second to Winstead and then stepped to a phone. No one else noticed until Winstead cleared his throat and made an announcement.

Chapter 38

Thursday 0500

Five minutes after the director of Homeland Security's whispered conversation with the national security advisor, the commandant of the Coast Guard contacted the commander of Coast Guard Station Dahlgren. The small Coast Guard base was located beside the U.S. Navy research base Dahlgren and lay between Washington and the speeding *Handy*.

The conversation was startling and brief. At times of stress, the commandant, outwardly an urbane, polished man, reverted to seagoing speech. "We've got to stop that fucking ship."

The base commander considered. CG Station Dahlgren was mostly an air base, flying helicopter search and rescue up and down the Eastern Shore. He glanced outside at the storm.

"We've got *James Rankin* tied up alongside the station pier."

"Well, get it out and ram the goddamn thing," said the commandant.

The station commander did not pause. "Aye, aye, sir."

As the commandant went to brief the director of Homeland Security, the captain of the Coastal Buoy Tender *James Rankin* was being hustled out of his berth in his ship's cabin, and the Dahlgren master chief sped toward the piers to turn out the crew. Within ten minutes, the lines hit the dock and the 850-ton tender began steaming out of the narrow channel toward the river, headed south.

Lieutenant Commander Doug Wallace, captain of the *James Rankin* for all of two months, grabbed the mike. With one eye on the radar, he said, "All hands, this is the captain, and this is no shit."

~

Dugan and Jonah passed the ladders leading down to the second hold and found the first by almost falling into it. Nearer the bow, the smoke was thicker, and visibility was close to zero. Dugan bumped into the safety rail around the ladder going down, and Jonah bumped into him. The ship leaned into another turn, and there was a loud explosion close by. Steel plates groaned and screeched, but the engine kept up its steady beat.

They were running out of time. Dugan tossed the blasting cap from the first bomb into the darkness below. Grabbing the handrail, he flew down the steps and smacked hard into somebody coming up, going equally fast. The next few seconds were a blur, but Dugan expected trouble, and the other man didn't.

Dugan slugged him as hard as he could with the muzzle of the H&K. Fired with adrenalin, he grabbed the man by the throat with his left hand, bending him over the rail until he gurgled and somersaulted into the darkness below. There might have been a crash a long way down, but it went unheard.

Dugan and Jonah bounded down the steps two and three at a time toward the bottom of the ladder. After what seemed far too long, Dugan hit the deckplates and stopped—too quickly. Jonah crashed down behind him, and they both fell over in a pile of arms and legs.

"Goddamit," Jonah hissed, and then roared a laugh.

Dugan fought the impulse to laugh too. The reckless madness still held them.

After thrashing around in the darkness, they got to their feet and fumbled for their weapons. The place they'd landed was pitch dark, but a dim red light glowed ahead from the ship's lanterns. Dugan worked toward it, feeling his way. He sensed Jonah behind him, trying to keep contact. Down in the very bottom of the ship, the sound of the sea rushing past was louder, and Dugan thought he heard a different sound that might mean the Handy had sprung a leak somewhere. As they moved, the smoke thinned out and visibility improved.

He was suddenly glad he'd left Cassandra next to a hatch and under armor. She might live through this, or at least her chances were better than theirs. Jonah nudged his shoulder, and Dugan refocused on the scene ahead. After a second, he saw it too.

They were in the forward hold of the ship at the lowest level, in a long, dark cave filled with hazy smoke. Looming in the red dimness around them, gigantic shipping containers threw shadows in the gloom. Ahead of them ran a long, narrow corridor between the containers, and in the distance, another light. The steady beat of the engine and the vibration of the ship's rush through the water resonated through the hull under their feet. The metallic groans of the shifting containers, stacked high and locked together, added another element to the cacophony around them.

As the two men cautiously stepped forward, their feet scrunching on the gritty deck, Dugan focused briefly on their surroundings. The impact of the explosions had ripped open several of the containers, and there were large paper sacks of sandy, cereal-like stuff spilling out into the walkway. Dugan knelt, swept up some of the coarse material, and sniffed it. Jonah loomed over him, huge in the dim light.

"What is it?" he asked.

Dugan struggled not to laugh. Exhausted and strung out, hysteria was just a giggle away. "Kitty litter," he tried to whisper at first, but finally just said it aloud in the noisy hold. "Kitty litter."

"No kidding?" Jonah replied. "*Kitty litter?*" Dugan could have told him it was gold nuggets, and he would have been more ready to believe it.

Dugan dropped the handful and stood up. "Some kinds of kitty litter emit a low radiation count when the customs people put Geiger counters on them. We have said for years that if somebody tried to bring a bomb in by ship, it would be in a cargo of kitty litter. Everybody laughs. But here it is."

"Damn," Jonah said, shaking his head.

They broke off and began moving very cautiously up the lane of containers toward the light, expecting every minute to be attacked from front or rear.

"Kitty litter," Dugan said, as his feet slipped on the grainy deck. "Sonofagun."

Chapter 39

The second flight of F-22s had advantages. The first flight's attack data was automatically relayed to the newcomers by sophisticated instrumentation, and the first flight's data included several hits. The weather below was clearing. From 22,000 feet, they could see a rim of light on the horizon, and the cloud cover below began to shred, giving their weapons systems and the pilots' eyes a better look at the target.

There was no slackening in the tempo of the aerial attack. As the last jet of the first flight cleared, the flight lead from the second screamed down, weapons hot. Tracking radars in several frequencies reached out for the freighter. But now two blips were on their scopes—the real one and a smaller one coming down the bay, closing fast toward their target. The airmen didn't recognize the second contact, so they kept their sights on the bigger return. They knew the stakes.

On *James Rankin*, once they were out of the channel and into the Potomac, the chief ordered most of the crew over the side in the tenders. They went, but they went reluctantly, and the chief used his best seagoing powers of persuasion to get them over the side. Now it was just Lieutenant Commander Wallace, Chief Schmidt, and his best helmsman who volunteered to stay at the wheel.

The captain himself tuned up the radar as the chief handed him the ship-to-shore phone. "It's the commandant," he said, as if buoy tender captains took calls from the commandant every day.

For two minutes, Wallace did little but say "aye, aye, sir," while the chief and the lone helmsman conned the tender out into the middle of the river. In ten minutes, they had the Handy on radar, and Wallace calculated closing vectors in his head as the two vessels charged toward one another at a combined speed of better than 30 knots. As they converged, he swore softly in the wheelhouse.

The rain eased up, and suddenly the Coast Guardsmen could see the bulk of the Handy ahead, the white foam around her bows like a bullseye in the dim dawn.

The Handy's helmsman was blind to anything outside the ship; his radar was gone, obliterated by the airstrikes. In the confusion and smoke of his cramped, armored steering compartment belowdecks he was wholly focused on his electronic charts, watching the icon that was his ship steam up the river at 20-plus knots. He knew he had only minutes to live, and his exaltation at the nearness of Paradise was tempered somewhat by the bitter, acrid smoke that made his eyes water and his nose run. His charts were the best on the market, he knew, and they showed the ship's progress with great accuracy—its location in relation to the channel and its markers, shoals, shallows, and fixed obstacles. They could not show him, though, the 175-foot buoy tender driving directly for the Handy's bows.

~

At the end of the corridor made of containers, Dugan saw a ring of low-power floodlights around a shipping container set by itself on the deck, chain lashings leading from the upper corners to deck rings in the shadows outside the lights. The end of the container was open; its massive door pushed back and out of sight.

As Dugan and Jonah watched, the ship rounded a shuddering turn and the door swung, slamming against the side of the container. Inside, lights bobbed around, as if several men were holding flashlights. Around the container, moving in and out of the circle of lights, six or seven heavies carried an arsenal of submachine guns. Dugan and Jonah had found the second bomb.

On a common impulse, the two men moved forward, staying well back in the shadows, crouching behind a lashed-down packing crate, and staggering a little as the ship swerved through another turn. As they moved into their new cover, there was a deafening crash overhead, and the ship shuddered and rolled from side to side. Dugan guessed there was now another gaping hole in the ship's armor, and he thought briefly of Cassandra under the hatch cover.

In the lights ahead, Abu Husam appeared briefly at the door of the container and rapped an order to a guard. From their hiding place, Dugan couldn't make out what was said, but he could see Husam's mouth moving, and the two men embraced. Then the guard straightened and headed aft, toward Dugan and Jonah. Husam watched him go, then went back inside.

Arming. He's almost certainly arming the second bomb.

The guard stopped to converse with one of the other men nearby. He turned his head to the other guard's ear, and for the moment, no guard was looking toward where Dugan and Jonah crouched.

Dugan put his mouth close to Jonah's ear. In the nightmare of sound around them, he had to shout to be understood. "The nuke's in that box. Husam's in there arming the damned thing. That guard's coming our way."

"So?"

"So we have to get in there and pull the damn blasting cap out. Like before."

"How we goin' to do that?"

"Kill those guys and then just yank the wires. That will pull out the cap. Best I can do."

"Okay," Jonah said. "That's all? Just kill those guys, yank the wires, and go home?"

There was a prolonged ripping, hammering sound above them; the Air Force was making 20mm cannon runs. *The top of the ship must be Swiss cheese by now*, Dugan thought. Unbidden, Cassandra popped up in his mind again. *Not now.*

"Piece of cake. Let's get on with it," Jonah said.

Dugan stepped into the steel corridor between the lashed-down containers. He sensed Jonah behind him.

There wasn't any time for cleverness. They just walked out of the darkness and started blasting. As Dugan's finger tightened on the trigger of the H&K, the guard and his buddy looked up, and Dugan got a flash of big eyes and open mouths. Then they were gone, hammered into bloody rags while the man next to them disintegrated in the boom of Jonah's big 12-gauge.

The other two died because they didn't move fast enough. They both went for their submachine guns, but Dugan's was up and theirs were strapped across their backs. He fired, taking out one man. A second explosion from the shotgun threw the other guard across one of the light sets, and he hung there for a moment before sliding to the floor, leaving a bright red smear on the surface of the light.

"Take their weapons and watch my back." Dugan dropped his H&K on the deck and grabbed one from the fallen guard; it was faster than looking for a full magazine.

He ran the short distance to the open door of the shipping container. As he burst in, he kicked over a canvas bag with Arabic lettering on the side and a squeeze-detonator fell out. Two wires led

227

away from the canvas bag into the blackness of the container. The safety was off, like on the earlier one. He paused to rip the wires from the detonator. All that mattered now was whether the little silver blasting cap at the end of those wires was in its firing slot in the bomb, where any stray charge or even a blow could set it off. Dugan charged into the darkness of the container on instinct alone and was immediately blinded by white light.

Without thinking, he pressed the trigger of the submachinegun, and the light went out, leaving Dugan deafened by the gun's blast in the enclosed container and blinded by the light and the muzzle flashes. He was silhouetted against the dim light of the container's open door, and on instinct, threw himself aside and down. A burst of fire ripped through the space where he had been a millisecond before.

No time to think. He was up and charging toward the muzzle flashes, his submachine gun forgotten on the deck behind him. Still deafened and dazed, arms and fingers stretched out to grapple the unknown figures behind the flashes. Dugan collided hard with another man, felt the other's face in his hands. Then they were down, punching and kicking in the darkness, frantic and murderous alike, tearing and ripping at one another's face, throat, and body.

It was the second time that night Dugan fought for his life, and the blazing fury of his opponent momentarily threw him off balance. They toppled over, clawing and kicking at one another's eyes and throats. Neither man had mercy. As they grappled, Dugan heard the roar and saw another blinding flash of light. There was the screaming and grinding of mangled steel, and the inside of the container dissolved into chaos. The deck tilted up, then down, and they were thrown from side to side as they punched and kicked each other in the darkness.

Fingers tore at Dugan's eyes. He levered his head back and chopped into a cheekbone, felt bone snap. Snarling and grunting, they smashed against the wall of the container. There was a loud

228

report, the body under Dugan stiffened, and the exhausted agent took advantage of his enemy's dropped guard to chop savagely where the neck should be. A cry, gurgling, and then limpness, and the fight was over.

Dazed, Dugan lifted his head to make sense of his surroundings when there was another rending, tearing explosion from the bows. Without warning, he hurled forward to crash into something metallic in the dark. Even as the ship shuddered and skewed, his body was somehow pinned down as if held in place by some force, then abruptly released. In the darkness, he was disoriented and confused, near the end of his resources, and he momentarily blacked out.

The sound of gushing water came to him first as his ears recovered, and he realized the engine had stopped. The steady beat that had been with them for hours was gone, and in the abrupt silence, he could hear the wheezing of his breath and the sound of inrushing water. The tilt of the deck to the starboard side slowly increased. Dim light was in the container, filtering through the open door from the great rents and gaps in the hull and topside.

As his vision returned, he crawled back toward the entrance of the container. Abu Husam sprawled where they had fought, mouth open and eyes staring whitely in the dimness.

Dead, Dugan thought through his exhaustion. *Gone to Paradise.* With what strength remained, he knelt and rolled Husam's heavy body over against the tilt of the sinking ship. He felt the burned, bloody mess on the man's side where the blasting cap had detonated as they fought, weakening Husam for Dugan's final blow.

Dugan took a deep breath to gather himself and stood up unsteadily. The slant to the deck was more pronounced now. He looked toward the door of the container to see Jonah backlit against the light streaming in from above, standing with his legs apart, facing aft, shotgun in his large hands. On the other side of the container, another body was shredded by a 12-gauge load of buckshot to the face. Dugan was dazed.

Blood was everywhere, and the deck continued to tilt. He turned to look forward again, deeper into the gloom of the shipping container. In the indistinct light, Dugan could just make out a coffin-like silver-gray container identical to the one on the second deck. It was still latched and locked. The bomb was unarmed. The blasting cap that Husam had planned to use to kill millions had killed him instead. Wearily, Dugan found the H&K, picked it up by the barrel, and moved jerkily out of the container.

Now they had to get out. Dugan and Jonah could hear the roar of water as they braced against the deck's increasing tilt. They nodded to one another, and Jonah jerked his head upward. The two men stumbled past the bodies strewn on the slanting deck and headed back down the long metal corridor between the silent containers. Slipping and sliding, the footing was now treacherous on the crumbled, soggy litter.

The sound of rushing water was loud in the hold, and water began to flow across the deck, picking up the kitty litter in a filthy, dirty scum. Here and there, blood joined the oil and dirt. By the time they got to the ladder, the ship's starboard heel increased further, and they were wet to the knees. Dugan tried to remember the water depth in the Potomac but gave up; the ship would go to the bottom, however deep it was.

White dots of exhaustion floated in front of his eyes, and the difficult hand-over-hand up the slanting ladder seemed like an endless climb with legs that seemed to weigh hundreds of pounds. They came to another ladder; Dugan was aware of leaning on Jonah's shoulder, and Jonah's arms were around his waist. As they moved higher, shafts of light from great tears in the decks began to illuminate the walkways ahead of them.

230

Finally, they reached the base of the ladder where they'd left Cassandra to hold the fort. In the gloom, they both saw the body in red foul weather gear sprawled at the base of the ladder.

No, damn it, no, Dugan thought through the haze that surrounded him. He took a halting step forward and turned the body over. A bearded face looked back at him, bloody mouth agape.

"Hey," a woman's voice called from above. "I nearly shot you. Is it time to go now?" There might have been a quaver in it, but Dugan thought it wonderfully strong, and he stood for a moment drawing in air and feeling a rush of thankfulness through his body.

Jonah cleared his throat. Dugan nodded and began to climb the last stairs with new energy. The vessel's list increased. They moved as quickly as they could up the slanting steps and found Cassandra on the platform, her back against the hatch, submachinegun across her lap. A moment, a tired smile, and a look told Dugan she was okay, and she took his hand.

I must look really wasted, Dugan thought. *Well, I am.*

Jonah pressed on up the ladder, threw the dogs, put his strong shoulder against the hatch, and it blessedly banged open, admitting a blast of cold air and pale dawn that left them all blinking. Jonah took the lead, but as he started to exit Dugan roused himself with an effort and shouted, "Jonah! Drop the shotgun! We'll have friendly company!"

Jonah stopped, nodded, and very deliberately laid the pump down on the ladder platform before he stepped into the light. Dugan dropped the H&K, and he heard Cassandra's hit the steel plating as well. They both followed Jonah, unarmed, squinting into the weak dawn, balancing against the tilted deck.

They emerged into the beginnings of a beautiful day. The rain and wind were decreasing fast, and the sun broke over the horizon on the Maryland side. After the rain and sleet, it felt like summertime. They stepped into a panorama.

The Handy was aground near the left-hand bank of the Potomac. She was barely recognizable as a ship. Her decks and upper works were torn into rips and jagged pillars of twisted steel. Her bow was mangled, and another ship seemed to be tangled in the wreckage forward. Over the bow of the Handy, Dugan could just make out deck cranes and the Stars and Stripes flying from a halyard. The half-sunken wreck of the Handy was heeled over to starboard as far as she would ever heel, lying on a mud bank whose brown waters washed over the starboard railing and roiled all around her in an ugly, scummy debris field of flotsam. Upstream they could see the narrowing river, forests, and houses on either bank.

The captain and his two companions from the *James Rankin* were leaning against the bridge bulkheads, battered but erect and waiting for pickup.

Chapter 40

Thursday 0830

The big screen in the Situation Room showed the wreckage of the freighter. The debris, twisted steel, and long slick of bunker fuel surrounding the ship trailed away in a downstream slick.

The president had reached his secure position. The congressmen and women and others on the evacuation list were still in their safe locations, and no one had yet sent the signals that would bring them back.

The director of Homeland Security had departed for Coast Guard headquarters. Harvey Winstead, the chairman of the Joint Chiefs of Staff, and the director of the CIA were all slumped in the leather chairs, jackets thrown off and ties loose. No one spoke. The most unfortunate official in Washington at that moment was the presidential press secretary, who refused evacuation. As a former newsman, he knew this was the biggest story of his life, but his job now was trying to nail down what the official line would be.

At Langley, the Air Force lieutenant general departed for the flight line to shake hands with his pilots as they emerged, sweaty and exhilarated, from their cockpits. The screens in the operations room were powering down.

Almost unnoticed, Sal gathered up his jacket and walked toward the door. A young airman opened it for him, and Sal walked into the gray dawn. It was still drizzling a little, but to the north he could see the edges of the clouds and blue sky emerging. Alone, he stood in the rain while his car came around. Time enough later for the after-action reviews and the finger-pointing. His cell phone buzzed, as it had been since the ship rolled onto the mudflat and no explosion had come. The Coast Guard would secure the wreck, and Dugan would check in when he could. Right now, Sal decided, he needed a little sleep.

~

Dugan wearily swept his eyes around the scene. A host of small boats headed toward the wreck, including a couple of utility boats from the Coast Guard base, a gray patrol boat from the Navy side of Dahlgren, even a red and white fire department boat with "Colonial Beach" emblazoned on its red hull. Dugan looked aft, where a bomb had finally penetrated the armor and destroyed the engine. Steam and black smoke poured from the hole. No one else seemed to be alive.

Dugan, Jonah, and Cassandra looked at each other, smiled tiredly, then as one accord, they faced out and raised their arms as far above their heads as they could, as if they were stretching, signaling to the Coast Guard. Once they were spotted, they sat down on the slanting deck, leaning back against a steel bulkhead and each other, Cassandra's head on Dugan's shoulder. He was beyond tired, but her head and tangled hair against his cheek felt good. Somewhere in the back of his mind, it occurred to him that after twenty years of being alone, there might be a great future in running a bed and breakfast on the Chesapeake. At least if he got invited, he might give it a try.

But there would be time for that later. Right now, he just wanted to sleep. In the distance, Dugan heard the beating of the helicopters that would be bringing the boarding party and take them away.

###########

Afterword

Nuclear weapons in the hands of stateless terrorists is the nightmare of our times. The weapons are simple to design, but the critical component—fissile materiel in quantities sufficient to achieve fission—has thus far been hard for terrorists to obtain. Bombs can be composed of two kinds of fissile materiels: plutonium or highly enriched uranium.

Plutonium, a radioactive metal favored by bomb makers because of its greater power, is dangerous to handle outside of special facilities. Highly enriched uranium, though less powerful, can be easily handled and transported. The "critical mass" required for a uranium bomb is only about 50 kilograms of highly enriched uranium U235. At the height of the Cold War, the Soviet Union was believed to be producing tons of U235 every year.

About the Author

Bob Killebrew is a mountaineer from North Carolina, a graduate of The Citadel. He holds advanced degrees in history and international relations. During a thirty-year Army career, he fought in Vietnam alongside Montagnard tribesmen and Vietnamese paratroopers, commanded a battalion in the storied 82nd Airborne Division and a joint task force in Central America, served in the Pentagon at the highest levels and taught at the Army War College.

After retirement, he consulted on defense policy for the Defense Department and civilian corporations and was a visiting senior fellow at a prominent defense-oriented think tank in Washington. He has been a Green Beret, a paratrooper, a crewman on ocean sailing yachts, a lecturer and authority on national defense issues, and an author of books and studies on strategy.

He and his first wife Pixie live and sail on the Chesapeake Bay in Newport News, Virginia.

CPSIA information can be obtained
at www.ICGtesting.com
Printed in the USA
BVHW041411251119
564771BV00012B/1406/P

9 781939 696526